We Write on Water

Also by David Ackley

Mystery
The Opinion Page
The Obituary Page

Magical Realism
Prospero's Staff

Historical Fiction
The Patent Clerk's Violin
The Language of Equals

We Write on Water

David Ackley

Rain and Breeze Books, LLC

MOSCOW, IDAHO

We Write on Water/ David Ackley. -- 1st ed.

Library of Congress Control Number: 2023914739
ISBN 978-1-950631-12-4 (Paperback)
ISBN 978-1-950631-13-1 (Ebook)

*This book is dedicated to Scott, Craig and Dan,
three friends confronting what life has dealt them
with courage, perserverance, and humor.*

And this our life, exempt from public haunt,

Finds tongues in trees, books in the running brooks,

Sermons in stones, and good in everything.

—William Shakespeare, *As You Like It*, Act 2, Scene 1

Part I
An Unintentional Slip

Chapter 1.

As cold as it was this evening, Ron thought he would rather be out there on the dark, frozen lake than here in a stuffy room filled with people he barely knew. The bank of windows reflected dozens of animated figures and he had no chance of glimpsing the wintry landscape unless he walked up and cupped his hands against the glass. A caterer swung by with a tray of champagne flutes, and Ron, again, obliged his offer.

Ron had claimed to have forgotten the event with the hope of a possible escape route, but with Sara's continual reminders and excitement, they had both known that it was a failed ruse.

"You're not dressed yet, Ron?" Sara had asked as she'd tilted her head to examine her earrings in the mirror, holding up a necklace to ensure that it was a satisfactory match.

"Oh, is that tonight?" he'd asked.

With the beginnings of frown on her part, he'd stepped up and given her a peck on the cheek, "Just joking, Hon. I'll be ready in a sec." He sometimes wondered how she put up with him.

He would have begged out under normal circumstances, but this was a big event for Sara. She was to present the Nurse of the Year Award to a member of her own unit at the University Hospital's annual Christmas party, and it was a chance for her to enjoy time with her colleagues away from work.

Ron had gamely dressed for the occasion, donning street shoes rather than the insulated boots he normally wore on such a frigid winter night. He'd warmed up the car for Sara, and then the two had made the short drive in relative comfort, except for the nervous pangs in Ron's stomach at the thought of being thrust into a crowd and trying to make polite conversation. The Pyle Center had been a glowing beacon throwing its light out upon Madison's Lake Mendota as they'd parked their car and hustled through the biting wind into the quickly filling event hall. After shedding their coats and clipping on name tags, Sara had been pulled away by two friends to prepare for the upcoming presentation and Ron had found himself alone next to a decorative ficus tree.

The mingled conversations and laughter that now flowed around him lulled Ron into a warm, muted space. He soon floated through the tall windows and out over and onto the ice. He had skates on and began long sweeping strides, feeling the sharp blades cut across the glassy surface and hearing the tearing sound with each stroke. He found a rhythm and soon saw himself as a worthy rival of Apolo Ohno or Eric Heiden as he raced along. The lake seemed endless with a frosty fog in place of the shoreline. There was no sound other than from his skates, and nothing could match his speed. Except for a crow, which was coming up quickly from behind him. Looking back, he could soon make out that what he'd taken for a crow was, in fact, another skater, clad in a black flowing cape, and skating with an easy grace. When the dark-clothed figure drew up to him, it then arced out, describing a large circle around him, doing so effortlessly as if he were standing still. As the circle closed and the skater matched his cadence at his side, he saw that it was Joni Mitchell, straight off of her album cover on *Hejira.* She reached out and took his hand. It was warm despite being gloveless in the cold.

The unexpected clinking of a glass next to a microphone jolted Ron as he found himself staring into space amid a bustling crowd. He shook his head, taking a moment to adjust, and then sought out Sara so that they could make their way to their table. Ron recognized a few of those in their assigned group, but only remembered the name of Maggie, one of Sara's best friends, seated the farthest away from him across the large round table.

With the first words of the first speech, Ron tuned out—though not to the same extent as he had a few minutes before—twisting his waterglass this way and that and watching how the ice inside remained relatively motionless as he did so. His thoughts drifted off and were this time focused on a familiar topic for him—the status of his writing 'career.' *Yes,* he noted to himself that even in his thoughts the single quotes would appear.

Sara was on a life path with a trajectory that had never wavered from when he'd first met her. The medical profession was in her blood, even though her father had been an insurance agent and her mother a homemaker, so her pursuit was not genetic, but inspired. Ron's 'career,' on the other hand, didn't pay a dime and so he'd needed to find other means to support it, suggesting that it was really more of an addiction. Whether or not it was also his life path, however, he'd begun to question as of late.

He'd compiled his first four collections of poetry with enthusiasm—but self-publishing was not easy, nor financially rewarding work, so he now found it difficult to continue with the same level of excitement as he'd felt at the beginning. To cut costs, he'd bitten the bullet and done everything himself: editing the poems until they were as perfect as he could make them; working with a software program to create the final presentation in book-ready form; learning a digital illustrator to create the covers; and then finally ushering the little beauties out the door. Now, he'd hit a wall. As the speaker droned on and as he watched his ice cubes melt, he found that this recent lack of motivation worried him. Lately, when the inspiration for a new poem struck, he more often than not squandered the opportunity—dallying at sketching out even the basics for a fledgling verse until the idea eventually wisped away into a vaporous trail he could never retrace.

Ron had read about a famous author who, in corresponding with a friend, had discovered that the same idea for a novel—plot, location, and characters—had presented itself to each of them. The first had sat on the inspiration, been distracted, and shelved the beginnings of a story. The second had, a short time later, taken the idea and run with it, resulting in a well acclaimed novel. Their theory was that inspiration was always out there just waiting for a vessel to fill. If one vessel wasn't ready, another would present itself.

He had always liked that image—that there were others who dipped from the same well, so to speak. That he was connected with other poets in a way that transcended the bookshelf and the digital marketplace. He also felt it was true that one only had to be receptive for the words to flow. His sticking point was in taking advantage of the moment when it arose. Sure, he composed poetry daily in his head, and tried his best to write down what he could of it. Unfortunately, he'd lately begun to worry about physical and psychical clogged arteries, having deprived the necessary oxygen from so many promising starts. In the literary world, he was the opposite of a nurse—he was more of a Dr. Kevorkian of poetry, ensuring that the inspiration passed on to a more apt vessel.

Chapter 2.

Sara had enjoyed the evening immensely and had reiterated several times how proud she was of her team. Ron had reassured her that her speech had been great, and that Michelle, the award recipient, had seemed genuinely touched by her words and the honor given her.

The late hour, welcome warmth of the house, and gala champagne had them both drowsy soon after they were home.

"What did you say to Phil?" asked Sara as they were getting ready for bed.

"What do you mean?"

"I was talking to Betsy and glanced over while you were chatting with him, and your face suddenly turned red at the same time Phil gave a wince. What was that about?"

"Oh, nothing, just another one of my jokes gone wrong."

"Oh," Sara said in a knowing tone. "The three S's, Ron…" as she pulled back the covers.

Sara obviously thought that he'd forgotten her little maxim for him: study the room, stay in your lane, and stay positive.

Ron had been seated next to Phil at the big round table, and had been proud to remember Phil's name before they'd started chatting. Phil had said that he had finally, with some relief, filed for bankruptcy. He was the owner of a local bicycle shop and had been struggling over the past few years to make ends meet. Ron had commiserated and Phil had said that he could finally move on from his business and was already working in a new position for the City of Madison while he got back on his feet. Phil was skinny as a rail from his daily bike rides. Dessert had come—a rich chocolate mousse topped with whipped cream. Ron had declined, but Phil had dug into his, and Ron had commented, "Looks like you can afford that," which meant one thing to him, but something else entirely to Phil, and his acquaintance had taken more than a mild offense.

Ron stewed about his faux pas as he tried to fall asleep, and this brought to mind all the gaffs he'd made with friends and colleagues over the years. He was recalling a failed joke he'd made about the groom during a wedding toast when he suddenly saw things from a completely different perspective. As he began to drift off, he composed a poem in his head to convey the gist of this revelation—which he would forget by the next morning.

In Passing

Before I go
I want to piss off everyone I know.
I want to go out with a one-star Amazon rating and
Be unfriended—even by the ads,
So that when my time comes, I can relax.
I want Stan to remember
when I broke the reed on his tenor sax.
Aunt Jane will recall when I used Uncle Joe's razor
on her precious Manx.
The entire losing softball team will only picture
The blown call I made at home plate—especially the
     pitcher.
Jerry will wince at the jape I made
That was taken as a jab.
And my first girlfriend the time I tried to kiss
her sister while she was off singing in the shower.
I want these all front and center,

Prime in everyone's mind.
Every slip, every sin.
And I do this as a favor.
When I go out
The less they mourn me
The more they really win.

Chapter 3.

RON TRIED to recall the poem that had come to him the night before, but could only remember a few phrases along with the main gist, and found himself too groggy to care about reconstructing it. He instead spent time blearily perusing the newspaper's front page when another idea gradually seeped into his mind. He looked around and snagged a scrap of paper from the stack used for making grocery lists.

> ~~morning groans at me.~~
> ~~trying to coax a drumroll~~
> ~~out of sticky mud~~
>
> mist-shrouded figure
> tries to coax a drumroll from
> the mud of morning

Ron then turned over the scrap he'd written these lines on and added:

> I'm soggy spring moss
> marooned in the center of December's
> crisp crunch

Immediately dissatisfied, he crossed out these lines and wrote:

> I'm soggy autumn moss
> surrounded by the
> step lively, crisp crunch

of invading winter

Initially, he'd intended to include this last bit with the lines on the flipside of the paper as the beginning of a longer poem, but decided to just leave the first three lines as a standalone haiku. *Not a bad start*, he thought, particularly liking the use of 'drumroll' to conjure up the image of an army bogged down in a hopeless cause. Rising for his third cup of coffee, the verse perfectly reflected his mental state this morning, having been sleepless since two a.m. and finally dragging himself out of bed at six with a minor headache.

Ron filled another half cup, adding a healthy splash of milk for his stomach's sake, and stared down at what he'd written. Worried that he'd scratched out the better poem, he quietly read both versions aloud, feeling how they came off the tongue and touched his ears. *What kind of judge am I anyway, since I'm the one who wrote them in the first place?* he wondered, returning to the common problem of not trusting whether his gut had the proper biota to digest the poetry he fed it.

Shrugging, he folded the wrinkled scrap and stashed it on the windowsill, hoping he'd remember it later. He then scanned the last bit of news in the morning paper, deciding to ignore the computer and its early a.m. overload of blaring headlines and continual crises. His brain wouldn't have been able to handle it. Yawning and reassembling the newspaper for Sara, he gathered the crumbed plate and the long-since stained coffee cup, set them on the counter, and then made ready as best he could for his day job.

Ron didn't bother to stop at home after work. He needed some fresh air, some room to wander, and enough time alone for a recharge. The University of Wisconsin Arboretum was the perfect place for this and had been his refuge ever since he was an early teen. Often after school, he had been in the habit of catching the Madison Metro Transit bus to Fish Hatchery Road and getting down at Carver St. to access the calm and peaceful trails that wound through the woods. Now that he was much older and owned a car, he could choose one of several different entrances into the arboretum and today's pick was the Wingra Springs parking lot just to the south of Lake Wingra and the Vilas Park Zoo.

Somehow motionless on a wavering wire. No. Somehow still, on a wavering wire.

Ron had noticed the bird clinging to a thin electrical line which fed an aging wooden light post, and the words had jumped to mind. *Definitely not,* he thought, *way too alliterative.* The pole was located at the far end of the small parking lot, just at the edge of the bare trees where a trail entered the arboretum. He'd stopped to admire the small falcon's own piercing observations of its surroundings. The wording for a new poem began to gel when he'd spied first one, then several more, orange-tinged Northern Flicker feathers that had settled into the dimples created by early-season footprints—now barely discernible in the crusty, windswept snow.

He committed to memory what had eventually crystallized into another haiku as he followed the familiar narrow, icy path in the dimming light, vaguely aware of his surroundings, but actually following the trail of his own thoughts. The holidays were fast approaching, along with customers' increasingly pointed demands for fulfillment of pre-Christmas orders. And then there was Sara's insistence on spending the holidays with her folks. If asked, his first preference was to spend time alone enjoying winter,

as on this peaceful walk. His second preference would definitely be spending time alone with Sara. And next, rank-
ing far above visiting Sara's parents, was posting his compositions and cynical insights on his blog site. The light on
the post was burned out when he found himself back at his
car, but the snowscape made the surrounding details all
still ghostly visible.

Chapter 4.

THE WINDOWS were frost-on-black when he returned home and unlocked the front door. After jumping back from a gust of cold air, Cocoa let him know how glad he was that the world hadn't ended and that there was dinner soon to be had. The cat rubbed Ron's legs vigorously as his human turned on the lights, stashed his outdoor gear, and then padded to the kitchen where he alleviated most of Cocoa's concerns with a bowl of moist cat food. Sara was on late-shift duty this evening, and Ron wasn't particularly hungry just yet—although he was thirsty, glugging a glass of tap water and then pouring himself a healthy serving of a Petite Syrah, grabbing some crackers to go with it before heading for the study.

Waking his computer, he signed onto his blog and typed out his little haiku before it was forgotten—the common fate of so many other mental compositions in the past:

American Kestrel

    slate blue winter cloud
    russet blotch marking sunset
    sudden freezing wind

He'd been slowly collecting poems for a fifth collection to put into print, thinking to name it *Ambedo*. The word's primary definition was the reflection of light off of snow or clouds, but it had lately inherited the trendy meaning of a melancholy trance—fittingly, a state into which he was prone by nature. Before committing his compositions to paper, however, he'd long before discovered that it didn't hurt to first post his verses on his blog for feedback, and he would then formally compile the often heavily reworked results. He'd posted another poem a few days earlier with no resulting comments and was curious to see if anyone had responded. He navigated to the previous page.

> Thank you, Wind!
> I soar, swerve, cut a curve.
> Thank you, Branch!
> I perch, cheep, bust a chirp.
> Thank you, Cone!
> I pry, pick, take a peck.
> Flit, flip, flap.
> I never saw the Cat.

Recent comments now appeared below this post, and he quickly went through and deleted the several ubiquitous robotic and troll droppings before scrolling through the few remaining entries.

> BL: Ron, I see what you're going for here. Some sort of Beatnik era rap, right? And it catches the quick movements of a bird? Still, this seems a little out of character... were you drinking too much wine again last night?

BL was Brendan Lange, a friend from grad school, now living as a ski bum and barista in Missoula, Montana. *Such was the way with blogs,* thought Ron, reflexively reaching for his glass of wine. He'd started his website as a means of marketing himself as a serious poet, and he could have excluded all comments from his pages, but he'd been eager to see what others thought of his verses. Soon, however, some friends had joined in as followers, and the over-familiarity of their posts was creating the opposite of the image he'd hoped to project. Still, they were friends, and backing away from accepting comments seemed to be the wrong direction for the arc of his attempts at publicity. So, he responded positively just to placate his pal, Brendan.

Poetriter: You did get it, BL. And the Cat, as in hepcat?

Even though that wasn't what he'd meant at all.

The best poet and writer-related blog and website names had been taken by the time he'd started posting, especially those with 'poetry' or 'writer' in the title, so he'd come up with Poetriter's Blog, since he was both a poet and a short story writer. He was now convinced that Poetaster's Blog might have been a better choice, had it not already been claimed. He scrolled down to the next entry.

StanzaGuru: Hey, Poetriter, ignore BL. He must have dropped a downer this morning. It had a certain peppy rhythm that caught my ear. Keep 'em coming!

Ron didn't know who StanzaGuru was, but he envisioned an aging hippy, plugged into both his blog and a bong. StanzaGuru's comments were always positive and kind, and Ron had seen some of his thoughtful insights show up on other literary blog sites. However, Ron still wasn't sure how much the posited hippy actually dug his poetry, or if he was just being nice. It had occurred to Ron that the man could possibly be a poet himself, publishing under his actual name and blogging under the tag of 'StanzaGuru.'

Ron's phone vibrated and he saw on the screen that it was his uncle calling.

"Hi, Ron, I wanted to see if your holiday plans had firmed up yet. Natalie and I would love to have you two over for dinner on Christmas—if you're not going to be in Galena, that is."

"Hi, Uncle Paul. No, I think Sara is set on seeing her folks and so we'll definitely be down there for Christmas. When we leave depends a lot on work, but I'd say that Christmas up here is out of the question. How about sometime around New Year's?"

"Sure, we're flexible. I'll be out of town in the second week of January for that writer's conference in Ames—which you should go to, by the way."

"Well, you know me and crowds, Uncle Paul."

"Yeah, but the exposure would still do you good, Ron."

"How about, 'I'll think about it?'"

Ron could sense his uncle shaking his head through the connection. "OK, well, if you change your mind, you're welcome to join me. Hey, say hi and Merry Christmas to Sara for me, will you?"

"Will do, and the same to Natalie. See you when we get back, and Merry Christmas."

"Same to you, Ron."

His uncle Paul, a professor of English literature at the University of Wisconsin, was like a father to him. That meant, as in many father-son relationships, that they had a problem with either being too close with, or too distant from each other. Ron felt that they had finally reached some sort of stasis on a personal level. It was, however, awkward having someone who specialized in modern American poetry for a relative.

As Ron focused back on his blog, he realized that his academic uncle's opinions and commentaries on Ron's poetic attempts had evolved over time. Early on, Paul had given Ron mere platitudes, not taking his writing seriously at all; then had come the teaching phase during which he'd tried to turn each poem into a lesson on ways to improve; and then he'd remained more diplomatically neutral after Ron's negative reaction to the teaching phase. But lately, Uncle Paul had begun giving guarded complements, which made Ron even more nervous about his own poetic skills.

The last comment was from Georgio.

> Georgio: Poetriter, your poem was good. It put me in a happy/sad place. Can't wait to read another of your rants or short stories though.

Ron suspected that Georgio was really a teenage girl, based on prior responses. But he didn't care—at least a few people were actively following his postings.

Others often chimed in and had come and gone over the last several years, but these three and Sara were the current core followers. He had occasionally garnered interest from newbie writers—who had obviously found his name and status non-intimidating—and in the past had agreed to review their poems, providing his own assessments and advice while remaining as upbeat as possible regardless of the quality of the work he'd received. But something in him had recently snapped. Ron had lately slid into a deep pessimism regarding this entire poetic endeavor and was, he thought, justifiably unsupportive of those just entering the game and correct in warning them off. He found himself on the brink of ceasing writing and closing his blog site at the end of the year, finally abandoning the unfulfilling undertaking altogether. Or, at least until the itch to write became too great to ignore again.

Ron could easily trace the course of his downward spiral of author-related self-esteem. He had initially embraced the view a fellow writer had expressed to him at an ill-attended book signing in a small bookstore years back. He had been so impressed by her analogy that it had been one of the first things he'd related when he'd begun blogging. She had said that each book was like a little paper boat that you set out on a lake, and there was no telling whether it would reach a living soul or sink in the waves, and that if it did reach someone, whether the fragile craft would be picked up or have rocks tossed at it. This detached perspective had saved him from the agonizing pins and needles he'd usually experienced while awaiting the arrival of a favorable review—or any review at all, for that matter. And he'd also relied on the words of Georgia O'Keeffe. The painter had reputedly once said, "Whether you succeed or not is irrelevant, there is no such thing. Making your unknown known is the important thing— and keeping the unknown always beyond you." This quote had both mentally buoyed him up and caused him to dig deeper for the precise words that would capture the pure underlying meaning in each line he wrote.

But time and anonymity had worn him down, especially over the past year, and he now felt that his little boats had all sunk, and he was tired of searching out those mysterious unknowns. The image that gradually replaced those initial positive ones was that of a failed NASA mission—all of that time, money, and effort fired into empty space with absolutely nothing to show for it—no radio signals returned from the void. His mother and father never had the chance to read his poems; his boss, Toby, had lost and never read his signed copy of *Sonic Poems*—a collection Ron had dedicated especially to him; his uncle had only recently begun to provide honest assessments; and the reading public lay uniformly silent about each publication. So, the only honest feedback Ron received was through his blog, and given the lukewarm reception there,

Ron now had to accept that it was perhaps the quality of his self-published work, after all, which didn't live up to some underlying and unspoken standard. And that realization naturally assailed his fragile sense of self-worth as a poet all the more.

Still, he did have a backlog of poems and rants that he had decided to post by year's end, and he expected to leave the website up into February or March before pulling the plug. He was not continually depressed by the prospect of ending his writing 'career,' only melancholic, and fatally realistic about it.

Opening an empty document in his word processor, he turned to a matter that spoke more to Georgio's request. He'd written and posted musings or rants about the publishing process, and found them to be satisfying, purgative additions to his blog. On the drive home from the arboretum, he'd learned through a radio news program that a bone-headed senator had just secured a major book deal about his experiences while doing—precisely nothing while in office, in Ron's opinion. Hearing the report, Ron was like a fish rising to the bait and had composed a mental tirade by the time he'd parked his car between the two snowbanks marking his driveway. He knew that he should stick strictly to poetry and fiction and that he had undoubtedly driven readers away with these petty indulgences, but he simply couldn't help himself as, with so many things, it felt good just to let it out.

Before he began typing, Ron went back to the kitchen and heated up some leftovers from the previous evening's chicken stir fry, bringing the hot plate back with him to the study. He took bites between phrases.

There is a hierarchy, fellow poets and authors, and the vast majority of us are at the bottom of it—the peons. The mud sucks at our boots or bare feet as we plow the fields, the potato sacks are heavy on our backs, and our hands are raw from packing straw and mud into a timber frame house we hope to eventually call home. The walls are thick and solid—begun by others long ago and we get to add our own muck to it. If I've mixed some metaphors here, that is a punishable offense, but that's not really what keeps me at the bottom with the rest of you. That house we're building? It's the framed fiction that it's possible to get noticed and picked up by a publisher, or become noticed after we publish on our own—and we all feed into this fiction and help reinforce it with the hope behind everything we write and submit.

I have more to say about the process, but this post is really about celebrity and authorship. I'm generalizing here by saying that whatever it takes to achieve public notoriety depends on a great deal of extroversion, and whatever it takes to become an author requires a great deal of introversion. Something propels those with a certain propensity into the limelight—actors, politicians, music performers, internet influencers, Youtubers—and they are all good at what they do. However, with the possible exception of the musicians, this doesn't mean that they know how to write.

Now, take a look at new book deals and book announcements, and you might notice that a large section is comprised of—celebrities. A few might possibly write decently, or many may have good ghostwriters, but still, regardless of quality, they get the attention, and you don't. They get the book deals. So, if you want to sell books—get popular first. Then think about writing.

With the cult of celebrity, almost anyone in the public eye can get a book deal, because the publisher knows that they already have the required name recognition, and the book will sell on that alone. This is fine, and more power to the celebrities, after all, they need to use their fame for something, but the problem is that it crowds the rest of us out. If you are an unknown author, this lack of available shelf space further reduces your chances of getting published.

So, don't stop harvesting, winnowing, grinding, and refining the grain that results in that luscious loaf of bread, that work of art. Just be happy in the task itself, in the finished product, because it will likely never leave your own little cottage and make it into the market of that big, beautiful world.

Disclaimer: You all know I self-publish and if you are new here, please read my previous posts about the experience, and the reasons I chose to do so. I am also aware that posts such as these further sink my own chances of finding a traditional publisher.

After he uploaded this rant, he also bumped his initial post of his observations on publishing up to the top of his site.

Your book is precious. You magically brought it to life after shaping and nurturing it into being the best it could be. But please don't expect anyone to notice—that would be a big mistake and possibly inflict a large bruise on your tender ego. For a little perspective, consider this: there are more than 4,000 books published daily—that's published, not printed—which amounts to 1.5 million books published each year in the United States alone. In a community of 4,000 you might stand out if you were special enough. In a bustling city of 1.5 million—not so much.

One and a half million individual titles a year bears repeating. That is a hell of a lot of books, and there are only so many readers out there who will buy only so many books in a year. And, those readers are going to be enticed by the big publishing houses who have the weight of marketing behind them—the glitzy ads, the sparkling reviews, the prime shelf space—and you don't. I don't either, and so I'm writing this from experience.

And what are the main fiction books published? Romantic Fiction and Erotica. If you're not writing a bodice-ripper, you are already down a peg. Next in line? Thrillers or Sci Fi, and it's downhill from there. I hear Poetry sales are up this year, but I'm a poet and haven't heard any knocks on my door.

This might sound like sour grapes on my part, but no—as with everything I post, I'm writing this for you, the doe-eyed neophyte clasping your tome to your chest in which beats a happy, expectant heart. I just want you to enter this world that is new to you with some foreknowledge of the psychic perils that lie ahead.

Ron stared at this text that he'd posted more than two years previously and thought for a moment about deleting it entirely. *Maybe it's better for some of us if we never make the big leagues, anyway,* he thought. He'd self-published his first collection with high aspirations, envisioning adoring fans, chumming with fellow big-name poets, giving readings and interviews, receiving awards, and ending his life humbly admired. However, aside from poor sales, his first and only public presentation had lowered his sights significantly. The reading at a local library had been a disaster. He'd stammered his way through the reading, mispronouncing several words in the process. The Q&A had been even worse. Asked about the inspiration for one of his poems, he'd drawn a total blank and winged it with a lame answer, and when questioned about an earlier short story he'd authored, he could barely remember that he'd even written it. From this experience, Ron had relearned something that had become apparent during class presentations in his college days: that he feared, hated, and sucked at public speaking. So, there was a hidden benefit to his anonymity on the literary scene after all.

He decided to end his blog with a little humor, something he'd composed at work a few days before.

Just for fun

Oh, he was mangling mean.
He was the sort who would tear the winds off
    Oklahoma just for fun
Tie a burning branch to a hiking trail and watch it
    twist and wind away
Poke his finger straight into a hurricane's open eye
Needle a skyscraper until it ran back up its stairs
Hold up traffic by a mile and threaten to drop it
Grind his heel on a beach until it was shore
Yeah, he was just that ornery.

Chapter 5.

AFTER PUTTING up with increasingly frequent meowing, Ron stood up from his desk, and that was Cocoa's signal to trot to the front door. Cocoa was an indoor cat, but his domain during three of the four seasons was the screen-enclosed front porch. So began the winter dance. Ron would open the door, the cat would advance half-way out and stand there, sniffing at the cold and stiffening at any wind gusts. If Cocoa did go out, there were immediate cries to be let back in. This snipping cold was not to his liking.

Ron cracked the door obligingly ajar for Cocoa to pop his head out, but Sara's simultaneous opening of the exterior porch door caused an immediate back-arched leap of retreat by the cat. "Hi, Babe," said Ron as he pulled the door open wider for her, along with a fog of frigid Wisconsin air, to enter the living room. "How was work?"

"Oh, fine," said Sara, giving a shiver as she shed her coat and boots once inside rather than out on the frozen porch. "Mom called me two times during my shift, so that was a bit of a pain, but things were pretty quiet on the ward otherwise." Sara was a supervisory nurse at the University Hospital on the western edge of campus, the same hospital where she'd earned her nursing degree. She'd always said that she couldn't leave Madison, what with being able to walk out to Lake Mendota's Picnic Point every day, but this benefit was never expressed during the winter months.

"Why'd Gladys call?" asked Ron. "Everything all right with your folks?"

Sara began to explain, but then stopped and gave him a frown. "Now, Ron, don't go off the deep end, OK? She wants to know who to invite over for an open house on

Christmas Eve, and she also wonders which of the parties we want to attend from the many invitations she's received."

The alarm bells had started in his head the moment Sara had said, "Now, Ron…" and he'd decided not to take part in this year's festivities by the time she'd finished. But this position would likely change during the upcoming negotiations.

"It's funny. I was going to tell you that we're totally backed up at work, Honey. I think I'll need a couple of extra days from when we'd first planned before we head to your parents'… but now that will sound like I'm trying to get out of going…" Which he could tell was exactly what it did sound like to Sara.

"I know it makes you uncomfortable being around all those strangers, but they're old family friends, and you almost always end up saying it wasn't so bad afterwards. Especially if you've had a few. Remember you enjoyed talking with Mister Highsmith two years ago? And Ms. Morgan, the retired music teacher? They're both coming. You have to go, Ron. You promised!"

"Don't worry. I know I did, and I will," he replied. "Only, I think I have to miss a day or two at the beginning. We can go in separate cars."

"Well, I'd rather we go together, especially in this weather. Mom's counting on me to help out the minute we set foot in their house, and I can't very well say we need to wait a day without a major snowstorm or a global pandemic for an excuse. Besides, I'm finally going to have some vacation time and I don't want to waste a minute of it."

"OK, OK, I'll talk to Toby and see what we can work out." Ron paused before he said the next bit. "And, I was hoping for a couple of days to get my blog in order before I put it in the deepfreeze."

"Deepfreeze?" asked Sara. "What are you talking about? Your blog is your life."

"Not anymore," said Ron quietly. "I've decided to take a break from this whole writing schtick. I'm wasting time and money that we can use on other things… like the wedding for example. Afterall, it's not like I'm getting paid to do it through my fantastic sales, and it just isn't fulfilling for me anymore."

"Not fulfilling? It's all you think about, Sweetie," said a perplexed Sara. "You've been writing since I've known you, and it's who you are. You can't just quit."

Ron looked down and watched Cocoa head toward his food bowl. "It's several reasons at once, but I need to at least take a long break from writing. It's just too… ungratifying, like I said. Anyway, I thought I'd upload some poems I've been sitting on onto my site just to give them a chance to be seen, and then pull the plug after Christmas."

Sara had witnessed Ron's ups and downs—both during the writing process, and while he waited for the feedback to arrive. The most obvious mountains and craters always came after he'd sent his books out to literary agents or reviewers to see if any of them would pick them up, which they never did. She'd come to dread the times when he'd giddily announce that he'd finished his 'best book yet' and was going to send it out to agents. She'd learned that there would be weeks of tiptoeing about afterwards. Especially if this happened during the darker days of winter.

"Don't be rash, and remember that your therapist thinks that your website is very beneficial for you. Why don't you see how you feel after we get back from Illinois? It's all the stress of the season. I'm sure of it."

"Yeah," said Ron.

"And make sure you talk to Toby at work tomorrow and find out about the schedule and urgency there. You know, he should hire more help, especially at this time of year." Sara started for the kitchen. "Any stir fry left?"

Toby, Ron, and Stewart were the main employees at Crone Amplifiers. Toby and Ron had been dormmates in college, and they'd built a guitar amplifier together as an experiment—a forced endeavor since they were severely cash-strapped at the time and couldn't afford to buy a new one, or even a good used one. For Toby that was the spark to pursue a degree in electrical engineering and start up the company. For Ron, the English major, his love was in the tubes and construction of the circuits.

Stewart built the external cabinets and took care of all the finish work and final testing. Toby ran the business and, when time allowed, installed the speakers and the power units into the cabinets. Ron soldered the power units and the tube amplifiers. He loved his job. Where most people would be bored to tears at the repetition, Ron found his happy place in the continuity, the melting solder, and the completed units. It was a space where his hands could stay busy while his mind was free to think his thoughts and compose more poetry. The circuits and the words both found their own cohesive paths by the end of the day.

"Yep, in the fridge," he replied as he followed her into the kitchen.

"How about England, or Ireland?" asked Sara as he settled in across from her at their small dining table, joining her with another glass of wine. He and Sara had been together for ten years, with a few breaks, and had always seen marriage as a mere formality. However, as they were approaching middle age, both had agreed that having the certificate would greatly simplify taxes, insurance, and health coverage. So, as an excuse to take a trip to the British Isles in celebration of something, they'd decided to have a small ceremony and cement the deal—small, at least until Sara's mother had become involved.

This house he'd grown up in was another reason for marriage. Ron wanted Sara to share in its ownership, but he couldn't extend an offer because he had no stake in it either. His father had left the house to his brother, Ron's uncle Paul, the university professor, with the stipulation that Paul retain ownership but let Ron live there rent-free, with expenses covered by a stipend to Paul issued from a trust Ron's father had established. Ron also received a small stipend from the fund, but the house was to remain Paul's asset until such time as Ron married—regardless of age—an apparent trigger showing that Ron had become responsible enough to warrant such a valuable possession. Yet another dig that his father had zero faith in his son, or at least in his son as he had known him when he died.

By the time they went to bed, they'd agreed on England—or Ireland, and Sara had convinced Ron not to close down his website in the new year. "It can just sit there, and it'll be ready for you when you're ready."

Chapter 6.

RON MADE breakfast and gave Cocoa some of the scrambled eggs as a sleepy Sara joined them. She was calm now, and they had a good chat over her morning coffee, but Ron knew that, as the minutes ticked away leading up to the Galena trip, she would become wound tighter and tighter. He was glad to be heading to work as the countdown began. He was washing up from breakfast when he remembered that Sara was guaranteed to devote her time, from now until they were on the road to her parents', to packing and to cleaning house—the place had to look showroom quality for Ms. Sarsgaard, the kindly woman from next door who looked in on Cocoa while they were away.

As he put on his coat, he called out, "Hey, Honey, I'm going to pop by and double-check with Ms. Sarsgaard about cat sitting Cocoa before I head to work, so at least that will be taken care of."

"OK, thanks, Ron. Remember, that might make you late," called out Sara from somewhere upstairs.

Ron knocked on the pink door and prepared for a long wait. Ms. Sarsgaard answered on the third attempt—a recent speed record. Arthritis meant that the startup was slow, but momentum was fine once she got going.

"Well, hey, Ronald," she said as she pushed the door open wider with both hands. "What brings you by then?"

"Hey, Ms. Sarsgaard, I just wanted to check that you were still good for looking in on Cocoa next week. We can find a cat sitter if that's a problem."

"Oh, no, no problem at all. I love that little kitty. Why don'tcha come in outta that cold?" gripping her housecoat more tightly around her neck.

"Thanks, but I really have to get to work."

"Well, we can't stand here with the door open. I don't need to heat the great outdoors."

"OK, just for a sec," said Ron with barely discernible regret.

Ms. Sarsgaard had babysat, and then become a second mother to Ron when he was young, and now took any opportunity to tell childhood stories about him that he'd rather forget. It was a joke between him and Sara that Ron always had to act like he was in a rush whenever they handed her the keys—if, that is, a timely departure was to be had. Not that they didn't invite her over for dinner once a month, and for Thanksgivings and Christmases when they were home. Ron's mother had passed away when Ron was eight, and Ms. Sarsgaard had stepped in to help Frank raise his son as much as she could manage while minding two older children of her own. Her vision and hearing were recently failing, but her memory remained razor sharp.

"I was just thinking about that time your friend Scott and you got his car stuck but good when you tried to drive out onto the Odana Hills Golf Course. You called in a panic and Lars went and tried to pull you out. Do you remember that, Ronald?"

Oh, boy, here we go, thought Ron. "Yes, I think I do." He said diplomatically.

"And then Lars got stuck and you had to find a tow truck before the police came..."

The story lasted five minutes, during which time Ms. Sarsgaard sat down and drank half of her cup of coffee. Ron noticed that muted morning soaps were playing on a small TV in the corner surrounded by ribbons, plaques, and trophies her sons had accumulated over the years.

"So, what's Lars up to now?" asked Ron when she'd finished. Lars had been into hot cars and hung out with a rough crowd in high school. He'd later served some time for running a chop shop, but the last Ron had heard he was attending a community college in Kenosha.

"Ya, sure, he got himself a job last month at that Oscar Meyer."

"Oh?" asked Ron, picturing an older Lars on the hot dog assembly line.

"Ya, he said that he's a Senior Brand Marketing Manager. I'm real proud of him."

"Yeah, you should be," said Ron as he sidled to the door and made his goodbye. *Lars, a manager in marketing,* thought Ron, again aware that one could never tell where life would lead. As he walked down the steps and toward his car, he also realized that he was feeling slightly jealous of the upward trajectory of Lars' life path.

Chapter 7.

CLASSIC ROCK music was perpetually blaring from the speakers in the shop, and Ron's remedy for this was to put on his noise-cancelling headphones as he settled into work, remembering now and then to tap his foot in time to the muted background beat. Neither Toby nor Stewart suspected that in reality Ron only listened to the classical/light jazz spectrum of music under his headphones where he should be tuned into the Gods of the Guitar given the business they were in. The current choice that matched his mood was a symphony by Phillip Glass. It wasn't that he disliked the shop music he heard whenever he had his headphones off. In fact, during his early teens Ron had devoured the huge record collection his uncle owned from that era, and he still enjoyed listening to those albums when he was able to choose them for himself. Unfortunately, however, listening to the Pandora stream of shop music had two drawbacks, the first being that listening to song lyrics was incompatible with poetic inspiration—unless one wanted to sound like the copy of a song, that is. The second drawback was that tuning into old hits was like Russian Roulette—after a session of pop/rock, he had no control over what would worm its way into his head only to reemerge at a later time, and he often found himself replaying the songs he had never cared for in the first place—over and over again. He'd rather be stuck in a Bach loop than Bachmann Turner Overdrive in endless replay on a sleepless night.

The shop was jammed with orders but none of the three of them could work at any faster pace than the groove they'd established over the past twelve years. Of course, anyone would love to see a Crone Amplifier sitting under the tree on Christmas morning, but with only seven to ten units at the most making it out the door on any given day, there were going to be many pictures of promised amps enclosed in cards this year. Toby's acceptance of orders had far exceeded any hope of meeting the yearned-for demand—as was becoming the norm. The spotlight trained on their company in the gear section of a prominent guitar magazine hadn't helped things in the slightest, at least as far as Ron was concerned, but Toby had been ecstatic at the free publicity.

Almost predictably, given the need for nothing out of the ordinary to occur during the holiday crunch, the morning hadn't begun well. "The new guy didn't work out," Toby had said matter-of-factly when Ron had opened the door to the small warehouse they were renting to the south of town near the Beltline.

"Kyle, the shipping and delivery guy?" Ron had asked. "Really? What was the problem?"

"It looks like Kyle made deliveries to several of his non-customer local friends and then skipped town," Toby had said morosely.

"Oh," Ron had said, with absolutely no inflection in his comment. It seemed that, try as they might to add staff to the company, it always filtered down to the three of them. "And at Christmas," again, flatly.

"Yeah, yeah," Toby had replied. "Don't bust my chops about it…"

"Bust your…" Ron had begun, and then took a breath. "Look, Toby, you beat yourself up all the time, and you know it. Don't blame me." Toby had looked over at Ron with a scowl but had then relaxed and nodded. "We've talked about this staffing thing before—we can either keep on at our own pace, or try to go big, which means either a major expansion, which I don't see how we can afford, or turning things over to a larger company. Magneto Amps is licking their chops over your overtures of us possibly joining them, as you're well aware. Myself, I think that would be a huge mistake. I like where we are. You just have to quit promising people the moon—especially during the holidays, for Christ's sakes. We don't need the pressure, and it just hurts our rep if we get months behind or start turning out crap."

Toby had launched into a stock businessman's reply about tooling up for the future, but in the end had said the words that were pretty much their motto, "Handmade is hand made."

There was a slight aroma of pot mixed in with the solder fumes being blown off his workstation as Ron began assembling the components he'd organized for the first amp of the day. The jumble included a main board, tube sockets, wires, many various resistors, the transformer, capacitors, jacks, switches, bulbs, etc. He was half-way through the second amp when he caught a snippet of a song playing outside his headphones, and he pulled them off to focus on an old tune by the Chieftains that was keening out of the area speakers. The plaintive song reminded him of Sara's and his plans for a possible trip to Ireland, and the melody carried him back to when he'd been on a short tour of the Irish countryside one summer after graduating from high school.

Suddenly it was as if he was in Ireland again, and the shop dissolved around him. He was reliving an intense crush he'd had on a roadside tavern's serving girl which had developed over the duration of a pint of stout and had lingered with him like the foam on the glass for the remainder of the bus tour and on the flight back home. The feeling from that encounter was unexpectedly reborn as a light tightness in his chest as he sat at the outdoor table waiting for the beautiful lass to reemerge with a tray of pints for the group sitting next to him.

Stewart dropped something with a clang that penetrated his reverie, and Ron was back at his soldering station. He translated the sensation of that day into a poem which gradually took form during the remainder of the amplifier construction. He lifted his magnifying visor while his other hand went for his trusty notebook and pencil, and he wrote the words down to post on his blog that evening.

It was a weird wobbled wave
But Colleen was brave
When she gave one.
It lapped at my eyes
And blotted the skies
For an instant.
I blinked back in time
Broke a half-moon smile—
A wee bit wan.
Her cheeks turned the red
of the sun that had fled—
my redemption.

Chapter 8.

IT WAS as he had expected. The dishwasher and washing machine were both whirring and swishing away when he opened the door. Sara was scrubbing a toilet when he said hello—her reply echoing back as if she were deep in the process, and when he went upstairs to fetch his slippers, there were two half-packed suitcases open against one of the bedroom walls. Sara was in leaving-the-nesting mode, and they still had another full day before they had agreed to head to Illinois.

Toby had said that they were so far behind at work that a day or two either way wouldn't make much difference to the backlog, but that it would be nice if they could pump out a few more amplifiers before Christmas. His friend and boss had a list of both the extremely irritated and those he knew personally, whose orders he had bumped up into priority status, but meeting even that smaller subset of demands would still have them working till Christmas Eve. As yet, Ron was undecided whether to stay a day or two extra and help with the last-minute push, or to bag it and leave with Sara on Saturday.

Ron had prepared dinner and, as they sat at the table enjoying the roasted potato and sausage meal set before them, Sara worried over all that she—they—had to finish before the trip, including her working a full early morning shift the next day.

"So, what did Toby think?" she asked, crunching on a bite of the side salad.

"Well, he thought we were behind."

"Um, yeah, you'd mentioned that! What did he say about your sticking to our agreed upon schedule?" emphasizing the words 'agreed upon.'

"He said that it was up to me, but that there was an A-list that he'd like to get product out to."

"Great!" said Sara, which surprised Ron. Knowing her partner as well as she did and the way he struggled to make decisions he'd expected her to say, "Oh... great," upon hearing that the choice was left up to him.

He nodded and bit into a potato.

"And so that frees you up, right?"

Ron nodded and to change the subject said, "Yeah, except for posting to my blog."

He looked up at Sara and saw immediately that this was the wrong segue.

"Which I'd better get to right after dinner."

"And packing and cleaning up?"

"Sara, there's still plenty of time for that—we have a whole day yet."

Early starter met continual procrastinator with a chilly silence.

Ron had relented by washing the dishes and cleaning the kitchen to Sara's pre-trip standards before hitting his blog. He posted the poem about Colleen and then searched his archived poems for some to publicize. He reread and lingered over one and then decided to post it. He had been out in the conifer section of the arboretum last spring and had stopped near a red pine to watch a red-breasted nuthatch descend, either absolutely heedless or completely uncaring that Ron stood within six feet of the little bird. He'd studied the nuthatch in its hunt for a meal and thought that it perfectly mirrored him in his search for the right words in a poem.

Nuthatch

I can't help it,
I was born this way.
I look at things askew,
Twist the upside down,
Probe crevices, poke punk
Until I sense it—
Pick and pry,
Try all angles,
Flick distractions.
And then there it is—
Something decidedly alive.
It shrinks back,
But it's mine.
That wriggling nugget that feeds me.

And then Ron became distracted, which was something that would never happen to a nuthatch. He'd come across a draft piece he'd written about the publishing process, and after spending some time editing it, he decided to post it as well.

From my pen to your eye. As intimate as tipping the quill to paper one last time, setting it back into the inkpot, delicately blotting the page, and then folding and slipping this missive under your door on a mild spring morning. That's how it should be—a straight line from me to you, dear reader. Unfortunately, I don't know where you live and haven't the foggiest how to get my words attractively packaged and distributed out to more than just a handful of you on my own. That's where the intermediaries between you and me come in.

If you want to publish your book, and decide not to attempt this on your own, you obviously need a publisher.

Like everyone else, publishers are trying to make a living, and they, naturally, are only interested in what sells. They don't have the ability to sift through over a million books a year to find the ones that might be profitable candidates for them to print. So, long ago, they cut off your direct access to themselves and began to rely on others to do the sifting for them—the literary agents. This has created the following short pecking order: you pitch to the literary agent, and then the literary agent pitches to the publisher.

Now, I know nothing about the process between the literary agent and the publisher, but based on what I've read, just because an agent likes your book, that doesn't mean that the publisher is going to pick it up and run with it. However, the process between the author and the literary agent, I do happen to know something about. And as a process, it is a failed system. Failed how, you might ask? Well, what would you think of a website where you enter in all the information it required and either nothing happened, or you were presented with a screen that said: Sorry, that information is incorrect, with no prompts as to what you had entered incorrectly? And where you only get one shot at it?

There are scores of sites and books that tutor us in the creation of the perfect query letter to grab the attention of a literary agent. (Yes, this letter even has a special, ironic, name.) With so many books trying to make it into the market, the agents are swamped with submissions, and many only open their doors occasionally, given the volume involved. From their perspective they are doing their best, and I know they are. But from the perspective of the author, the process offers zero chance for improvement.

You submit your query letter. You will then either receive a canned reply stating that this is not exactly what the agent was looking for, or you will receive no answer at all. That is pretty much it, and this is why I tagged the name as being ironic in the previous paragraph. In order to be classified as a query, shouldn't a reply be involved?

You certainly can't have an answer without the question to engender it. This might seem like nitpicking, but it is exactly the point. There is a plethora of information on creating the perfect query letter, but without any feedback, how does one improve? And how does one know whether the query letter was the problem? Was the agent simply having a bad day when they read your letter? Did they pass it off to an incompetent underling? Was it not the kind of book the agent was interested in? Was the letter good, but the excerpt from the book sucked? Was the letter bad but the book good, so based on the letter the agent couldn't trust your abilities? Did you not flatter enough? Too much? Was the letter worthy, the book worthy, but the agent knew that the publisher he/she was connected with wouldn't go for that sort of work?

You see the problem. The poor authors are blindfolded asses trying to pin the tail on a moving comet. There is no feedback loop for them to improve, in fact there is slim feedback at all. I praise the literary agents who have replied to my letters with more than a canned response, and curse those who provide no reply at all. There, I said it. Another black mark be upon me.

Posting this felt good, but rereading the diatribe had sent Ron into a minor funk. Rather than hunt up another poem, he went into the kitchen and uncorked a new bottle of wine, joining Sara on the couch where she had collapsed to watch an episode of *Midsomer Murders* before bed. He made it part-way through the program. He'd seen it before and had tuned it out while he stewed about his inability to market his own books. He was back at his computer and typing away when he heard Sara say she was heading to bed as most of the lights in the house went out.

He was midway through the next rant when he noticed that he had a comment on his most recent post.

Rn-TLC: I always love your views on the publishing industry, Poetriter, especially the ones that encourage those who are just starting out on the publishing path. It's great to have your warnings for us to heed, and I know that you write your pieces to help us stay aware that it is not all a bed of roses out there. But please don't post these at any detriment to your future as a writer. Someone like me is totally anonymous, but you are not. All of these essays reside on your website, and everyone knows who you are. Just my opinion, but positive is always better.

Hmm, thought Ron, and headed upstairs.

"Hi, Hon," he said when he opened the bedroom door and found Sara sitting cross-legged on their bed, hunched over her laptop.

"Hey, Ron," she looked up and smiled.

"Um, not totally anonymous. You usually just tell me your opinions on these posts to my face. What gives?"

"Well, Ron, I was reading what you just posted and thought about what a potential literary agent might feel about it. They might think twice about representing you if you're trashing them online."

"I wasn't trashing, I was just being honest."

"Yeah, but Honey, that's not the way they might see it. I'm sure those that..." She paused.

"Those that what?"

Sara took a moment to look into his eyes before she said, "You know, there are those who have been picked up by an agent who might not feel the same way about the process as you do. They might see it as the road to success. We've talked about that."

"And, we've talked about how good it is to not keep stuff bottled up," he countered.

"But there must be ways that don't affect your chances of success."

"I don't really think it matters, Sara. Remember, I'm closing things down."

"Well, all I'm saying is that if you just kept to the poetry and nixed the rants, you might not need to close down."

Where Ron would normally get wound up at this point, he had to admit to himself that she was probably right.

"Anyway, I stand by what I wrote and I'm not deleting it. I think it's helpful to some."

"Okay, that's fine, but just remember you might have a wider audience than just those few people who respond in person."

"The key word being 'might,'" shrugged Ron as he stepped up and kissed her forehead.

She slapped her laptop shut and pulled him onto the bed, and they adjusted positions so that they were lying face to face. She rubbed his arm and smiled at him. "Do you remember those blue periods you would enter into when you first started getting the rejection letters?"

"Yeah, my skin was way too thin back then. Why? I'm not sad now?"

"No, not sad," and Sara drew out another pause. "Not sad now, but I worry that you're starting to be a bit more… cynical, or maybe angry about the whole thing."

"I don't think I'm angry, just realistic."

"Well, Hon, reading your last couple of posts, I mostly pick up on some anger. You said that you're talking to Pete, your therapist, about it?"

"Yeah, Pete thinks that writing things out in my blog is a good way for me to deal with my frustrations in an acceptable manner."

"But do they help you become less frustrated, or do they stir you up more? I mean you haven't kicked the cat yet, but I can tell that you're more wound up than usual."

"Sara, I'm not wound up in the slightest," Ron said, a little more forcefully than he'd intended.

"OK, as long as you're aware—I just want you to be happy. Those posts might be good for you if Pete recommends them, but I still think they're bad for your online image."

Ron was about to pull away when Sara reached over and brought him in close. He could feel himself relax as they kissed and then they both quickly undressed to become closer still .

He awoke after a doze and remembered that he'd left on some lights and the computer. He slipped into a robe and quietly made his way downstairs. He was about to close things down when he noticed the half-finished essay. He tried to heed Sara's warnings, but just couldn't help himself—he had to finish what he'd started. He didn't notice at first that his relaxed mood changed the more he typed.

Marketing is difficult for introverted writers. Especially given the inevitable self-doubt. How can you really know if your book is any good if no one has read it, or has read it and not given you an honest evaluation? How can you stand up and promote a book while not at the same time feeling like a snake-oil salesperson when you only have yourself as the judge of your book's quality? Don't despair, there are plenty of people out there who are willing to market it for you, regardless of the product—for a price, that is. Thus, we enter the business side of being an author and it has nothing to do with writing.

Who knows about your book? Some of your friends and family. That's about it. So how to get the word out there? Marketing gurus tell you to create a pre-market buzz that will drive sales when the book is published. But that only works if you have a following in the first place—

and your friends and family already know about it. So, you can shout into the wind for all the good it does.

OK, I have a slight tangent here—when did a book ever go bad or become stale? Did you ever decide not to read a book because it was published two years ago? I didn't think so. Yet so much of the publishing world is centered on the book's release date. There is a push for the pre-release publicity. Just-published books are prominently featured in the rags. Most review sites won't accept a book that is more than a year old, and many will refuse to review a book published more than 3 months before. How did it come to this? "Oh, no, I refuse to read *Ulysses* because it is so old?" The reason is that everything is driven by the big publishers who build excitement for every one of their new releases to boost sales, and they can afford to do it and they have the audience to target. You don't.

How can the little guy compete? Well, there are plenty of services who (yes, remember that corporations are people now, too) are going to convince you that paying for ad space and clicks on websites will drive sales for your book. The only problem is that the conversion of ads and clicks to purchases is appallingly low, and so the outlay for the advertisements can't be made up for by the number of sales you make. The advertisers, on the other hand, are making out like bandits.

He wrote another paragraph below this one which kept changing and becoming darker with each iteration. For once he actually noticed his change in attitude. *OK, maybe Sara is right,* he thought, and just ended it there. He was about to shut down the computer and join a sleeping Sara, but then he was struck with the desire to wrestle his feelings of frustration out of the ether. This time the words flowed with few edits before he posted them.

Invisible Ink

I write my words in the air
Struggling to keep them there—
Waving, slapping at them to stay together like a
     madman.
But the nouns verb away
Scattered with the next careless breath.
I scribble on the last withered leaf
Red and—plucked off by Fall's first heavy flakes.
I write them on a firecracker fuse
just before it is lit,
And on crystalline frost
as the first warm rays hit.
I write my words in foam on the waves
Just as they meet the rocks.

His sleep that night was no better than his poem.

Chapter 9.

Ron had thought that Sara was a gathering storm before the holidays, but Toby was an absolute Level Five hurricane at work the next morning. The casually presented A-list he'd mentioned the day before had become a Code Red priority overnight.

"Ron, are you positive that you can't just join Sara on Christmas Eve?" he'd pleaded before Ron had even removed his coat. Ron could smell the sweat of panic on him—and it was only eight in the morning.

"Why?" asked Ron. "I thought that we were just going to do what we could against the mountain of orders and call it good."

Ron had only seen Toby in such a state two times before. First, when they'd agreed to offer their amplifiers through a major music equipment supplier, and second, when they'd needed to pull out of that agreement because they couldn't possibly meet the demand and still produce by hand.

"There are people knocking on the door, Ron, that's why. And I had two phone calls in the middle of the night last night."

"Who'd call you at that time?" asked Ron. If he found out it was one of their wacko politicians, he would walk out right then. "What's the big deal?"

"OK, Gil Freeman of the Feathertones wants one for his teenage son, and Senator Jaworski of Michigan has promised his son one, too."

"Are you kidding me, Toby? You're on speaking terms with Gil Freeman? And both of those guys have your phone number? And they would call you in the middle of the night?"

"Hey, I'm in the business, you know?" was all Toby said, shrugging his shoulders.

"So, you're saying the pressure is on?" asked Ron.

"Hella pressure," replied Toby as he headed to the bay where the speakers and cabinets awaited. Ron then noticed that his friend had started smoking again. Cigarettes.

Fantastic, he thought, already missing the gentler times of Sara's pre-travel mania.

Ron busted butt all day and they had nine finished amplifiers with three others nearly completed by quitting time which today was two hours later than normal. He didn't like to work this way. There was no poetry involved.

"Feeling better about where we are?" asked Ron as they were turning off the lights.

"Just a sec," said Toby, flicking open a call as his phone rang, and saying, "Hi, Justin. Oh, yeah, you're definitely next on the list." Ron quickened his pace to his car—because of the bitter wind and because he didn't want to hear any more at the moment. Settled in and waiting for the car to warm up, he still couldn't shake the rancid sense of urgency that had rubbed off on him.

Sara was abuzz and all Ron wanted to do was cop a buzz. He headed straight for the refrigerator and opened a cold Point bock beer while Sara rattled on about work and what remained undone before they scooted out the next morning.

All was made better by a seafood linguini and a three-bean salad which Sara had put together earlier when Ron had alerted her that he would be home on the later side. They relaxed some and caught up, during which time

Ron tried to convey some of Toby's state of panic, but he could see that he wasn't getting through Sara's firm mental deadline for departure.

"What if we took just one more day before we left?" he'd tried.

"Why lay that uncertainty on my folks? They have plans. We have plans. Ron, you said that a day or two wouldn't make any difference anyway. Didn't you?"

"Yeah, but I've been trying to tell you that we're under a lot of pressure at the shop now. Toby is about to pop a blood vessel and would really like an extra day or two out of me."

"So, what's he going to do? Fire you?"

Ron had just stared at her for a moment. "You know what? I forgot that I was going to meet with the guys before we left," he said as he rose and put his plate on the kitchen counter. "I'm a little late," he said, looking at his watch, "but I can still get in some time with them." He headed for the front door to don his winter gear, and a perplexed Sara followed.

"But what about tomorrow? You need to finish packing!"

"I will. This will hardly take any time at all. Besides—doctor's orders." Ron's therapist had insisted that it was good for him to fit in a scheduled time with friends outside of work and family. He got together with one old classmate and three newer friends he'd met through a now-defunct therapy group for socially challenged introverts on a weekly basis at a nearby tavern. Pete often joined them as well.

"But..." Sara sighed and begrudgingly said, "I know. And it is worthwhile, just not the most convenient thing to be doing right now."

"I know. I think it really does some good, though."

"And we leave in the morning?"

Ron took a breath as he zipped up his parka. "Probably," he muttered.

"Probably?" yelled Sara as he pulled open the front door and stepped out into the sudden chill.

⚜

He was banging the snow off his boots in the enclosed porch when Sara pulled the main door open for him.

"How were they?" she asked as he entered, doffed and hung his coat, set his hat and mittens on the small shelf next to the rack, and stuffed his freezing feet into his over-sized slippers.

"Fine, and the Packers were winning." he answered. After a pause, he added, "We had a great talk and it's a beautiful night with the moon out."

Not to be sidetracked, she blocked his path to the rest of the house and asked, "Well?"

"Well, what?" He knew his hedging was a mistake the moment he asked.

"Jesus Christ, Ron! You said that you'd let me know when you got back. We have to leave tomorrow morning, and you'd better the hell pack if you're coming!"

"Sara," he said in a placating manner. "I just need a minute to write something down. It's fresh in my head, and I don't want to lose it."

Sara glared at him. "Goddamn it, Ron. Now I think you just say that to avoid the conversation. How about a simple yes or no?"

"I'll let you know in a minute," he said as he squeezed by her and headed for the study.

"Aargh," was all that Sara could manage as she stomped up the stairs.

Ron closed the study door quietly behind him to buy some time. At the heart of it, he really didn't want to go to

Illinois, but the trip was expected, especially this year. Ron had joined Sara and her parents in Galena during most of the past ten Christmases, but he'd found excuses to stay home, leave early, or arrive a day or two late more frequently in recent years. Instead of becoming closer to his presumptive in-laws, there seemed to be a growing discomfort and awkwardness with each visit, and he was sure that he was at least partially to blame.

Emerging from his brief retreat, he'd hoped that lobbying for extra time in Madison would be easy, but instead the late evening ended with them all wrapped up in a heated argument held together with a bow of grudging familiarity. Sara wanted to take full advantage of her vacation time from her job at the hospital and maximize the number of days she spent with her folks, and Ron, without directly saying so, wanted to spend the minimal time with her parents that he could possibly negotiate. Sara had argued that she needed to help her aging father with the decorations and begin the plans with her mother for their upcoming, with a newly appended question mark, wedding. Ron had reiterated that he could use the one or two solid workdays which were necessary to finish things up at the shop, and that he needed to get his blog in order before he left.

So, that evening Sara had finished packing in a pique with the intention of driving off alone the next morning. Ron was to join her two or three days later, and on Christmas Eve at the latest. Unfortunately for Sara, her plans were upended late that night by an emergency staffing call, meaning she would be working the afternoon shift the next day—causing some slammed suitcase lids and tears of frustration which Ron's presence at that particular time did little in helping to staunch.

Chapter 10.

THINGS HAD become the equivalent of a three-car pileup at work. Toby was tailgating, pushing them from behind, and driving while exhausted. Ron was seriously thinking about hitting the brakes, but gripped his own wheel and kept his momentum given the pace of Toby and Stew. And, as road rage and speed set the scene for a collision— Stewart had suddenly spun out in a full 360 and ended up in a mid-afternoon snowbank. With Toby and then Ron plowing in right behind him.

Still fretting over his fight with Sara, Ron had pulled off his headphones at the beginning of the shouting match.

"You're not listening!" Stewart had yelled. "The glue isn't even dry on the Tolex yet, so the covering will blister as soon as they head out the door! We're going too fast!"

"No one will even notice!" Toby had shot back.

"Not notice the outside of an amplifier? What else is there to see?"

"It's the sound that counts anyway!"

Then Ron had weighed in. "Hey, Toby. It's the total package, and you know it. Otherwise, we'd send these crates out as wooden boxes. Kinda like coffins."

"Shut up, Ron." Toby had said. "I know looks are important, but we can ease up on perfect for the moment."

Ron had known Toby for so long that the 'shut up' comment was barely noticed by him. But Stewart was another matter. "Shut up, Ron?" Stewart had screamed. "What is this? A fucking dictatorship now? Who died and made you king?"

"Me! It's my company!"

"OK, boys," Ron had begun. "Let's settle down and play nice. We still have a deadline…"

"Not for me anymore. I fucking quit!" Stewart had declared, and didn't utter another word, gathering up his things while Toby had begun imploring him to stay. Toby's last-ditch efforts hadn't worked, and Stewart had walked out the door, slamming it behind him.

Someone in the background was singing that they would get a sentimental feeling when Toby had stalked over and turned off the stereo. "Goddamnit!" he'd exhaled. He'd turned to Ron and said, "Well, there's nothing for it. I'll finish the cabinets that we have," as he'd started toward the bays where Stewart produced his magic.

"Toby…" Ron had said as Toby had approached the stack of bare wooden frames. "Toby!" he'd shouted when his friend and boss had picked up some shears to attack a bolt of red and black Tolex. "Stop!"

Toby had turned to him, dropping the shears to his side, almost looking relieved that Ron had parried his assault on Stewart's domain. "How hard could it be?" he'd asked in a more muted tone.

"You know exactly how hard it is—that's why we hired Stew in the first friggin' place. You can do a lot around here, Toby, but you can't meet Stew's level of work." He'd surveyed the amplifiers that were ready to go out the door, and at those in various stages of construction. "You need to get him back soon, or we need to bail on the rest of the orders until he, or someone more competent than either of us, is standing where you're standing."

Toby had spent the next hour and a half on the phone, talking, pleading with Stewart in fits and starts, and answering several phone calls in the interim. Meanwhile Ron had finished the amplifier guts that he'd staged for what was likely to be the final amp of the day. Ron had realized with each soldered component how much he'd messed things up with Sara. Especially if this disaster was their last day of work at Crone Amplifiers before Christmas. Which it was. Stewart had finally agreed to come back to work—after the new year—and had told Toby that he'd nearly done this exact same thing over the previous two Christmases. He'd said that he loved working with the both of them, but that the pressure of the holiday demands was just too much for him. He'd also made Toby agree on terms and expectations for the next Christmas push.

Before his last call with Stewart, Toby had asked, "What do you think, Ron? Should I cave to keep Stew on, or hire some new talent who can take the pressure?"

"Are you kidding me, Toby?" Ron had asked in surprise. "How could we do better than Stewart?" He'd thought for a moment and then added, "Besides, if the pressure was any greater—I would have walked out, too. Sara is furious with me right now, and it was all for this?" gesturing at the disarray around them. Toby, for once, had an expression that bordered on contrition and was about to say something when Ron had continued. "You know what they say about an old car, don't you? If one part goes and it's replaced with a new, stronger part, that puts stress on all the older components. Something else is bound to give out, especially if the car isn't treated with a little respect given its abilities."

They'd then sat and, over a seasonal beer from the small company fridge, had a long talk about the future of Crone Amplifiers. Ron had zeroed in on the cause of Toby's angst—the pride of ownership. "Look," he'd said. "It's just like me and my poetry. Do I put all my effort into finding a publisher who will handle my works, but give up my total control of how my books look and how I present them? Or, do I continue on as I have with total artistic freedom, but no sales to speak of? Do you want to hand our amps over to a bigger company and lose your say in how they sound, how they're made and marketed? Or do we just face the fact that we can only be so big before we lose the soul of the company?"

They'd decided that there wasn't going to be a new old-fashioned way for Crone Amplifiers. They were sticking with the one they had.

Chapter 11.

RON PHONED Sara as soon as he got home.

"Hi, Hon," he greeted her when she answered with machines beeping in the background. "It looks like there's been a change of plans."

"Oh, no, Ron," began Sara with cynical chagrin. "Don't tell me you're going to be even later!"

"Nope. In fact, I plan on joining you and making the Jorgenson shindig tomorrow evening."

"You're kidding!" Sara was suddenly ecstatic. "Toby finally got in the Christmas spirit?"

"Nope. Stew quit and we had to shut down production and be content with what we had."

"Stew quit? Why?"

"Oh, he promised he's going to come back after New Year's, but he was frustrated that Toby was pushing us too hard. He wasn't going to be content with sending out crap, so he just walked out the door this afternoon."

"Well, I'm sorry for the company's sake, but I'm really happy that we'll be driving down together!"

"Me, too. I figured if we leave by noon, I'll still have plenty of time to wrap up my blog and get things in order. Maybe even fit in a little shopping before we go."

"Remember, we said no presents?" There was an announcement in the background, and Sara paused to listen. "Because of the wedding expenses?"

"I remember. I still want to get something for your mom though."

"OK, but nothing big, OK? Oops, I have a little emergency brewing here. I might be home a little later than I planned tonight."

"OK, love you."

"Me, too, Ron. So glad we'll be driving down together! Bye."

❦

Ron fed Cocoa and then settled into his desk chair. He reviewed the poems he hadn't yet posted or published and realized how many of them were about birds. *Maybe I should package a collection of poetry featuring them,* he thought idly, and decided to post a few before making dinner. He still felt a pang when he came across his short verse about a goldfinch.

> Hello readers. I will be taking a break from this site for the holidays and into next year—perhaps well into it. I hope you have a safe and fulfilling season of renewal as we've just reached the winter solstice. Below are some poems that I hope you will enjoy. I'm thinking of putting together a volume of these and similar poetry, so watch for that in the future.

He then posted one of the shortest non-haiku verses he'd ever written:

Because I promised you a poem

Brighter than all the Christmas lights I just stowed
    away
Yellow breast-up near a stake in the muddy garden

Kingfisher

I was writing and now –
Where are all those words?

The ink is gone, spilled into
All murky browns in this dim light.
What was I trying to say?
It is so quiet here, so still.
I feel like I'm floating.
Where is that party of birds?
They seemed so boisterous a moment ago.
That sky has shrunk.
I'll just rest here.
Something is niggling away –
I come up
EMPTY!

Ron's phone buzzed and he dug it out of his pocket, glanced quickly at the screen, and then answered, "Hi, Nathan."

"Hey Ron, how are you doing?"

"Good. Trying to get into the Christmas spirit. How about you?"

"Great. Enjoyed Hanukkah, and getting ready for the rest of the holidays, too. How's Sara?"

"She's good. We're going to spend Christmas with her parents, as usual. She was planning to head down yesterday by herself, but was called into work today. I wasn't ready then, but now we can head down together tomorrow."

"Sara's an early starter, isn't she? And I know how you put things off till the last minute, too," Nathan said with a chuckle. "How are Pete and Gladys doing?"

"Same old, same old," said Ron. He decided not to tell Nathan that he and Sara were finally getting married and were going to polish up their plans when they were in Galena. He'd tell his friend about it after they got back. "Pete's starting to have some trouble getting around, but

Gladys is still hanging in there. Sara's worried about them as they get older, but they're fine, really."

"I hope so. Tell them both hi for me when you see them, will you?"

"Will do." Ron could tell that Nathan was leading up to something. "So, what's up?"

"Not much. Hey, did you catch me on NPR last weekend?"

"NPR? Really? No, I missed it. What was it about?"

"Oh, they were doing a retrospective piece on Robert Bly after he passed away last month, and I was invited to be part of a panel discussing him and his influence on Midwest poets. We each read some of our own works too, so it was good exposure."

"I had no idea. I'll have to check out the NPR website for a replay."

"Sure, Ron. Hey, I've been following your blog and see you have some good stuff coming out lately. The reason I called is that I'm going be doing a stint to promote *Winterberries*, my new poetry collection. I'm gonna start here in Minneapolis, hit Chicago, have a few readings in Colorado—Denver and Boulder—then on to Austin, and some of the West Coast. The highlight for me is going to be a talk at the City Lights Bookstore in San Fran. After that I fly back to Chicago and then head to New York and the East Coast. I was thinking that you could join me, and I could introduce you to some folks and drum up some interest in your work. What do you think? You could hook up with any part of the trip that you wanted."

"Wow, that's really generous, Nathan. Not sure I could rub shoulders with the type of people that you're going to be hobnobbing with, though."

"Hobnobbing, schnobnobing," said Nathan with a laugh.

"Schmooze, schschmooze," Ron retorted, as a common joke between them. And then, "Well, I don't know, that's a pretty big decision. I'll have to think about it and talk it over with Sara. How about if you send me your itinerary, and I can see if that could work?"

"Sure! I just thought that it might be fun to share some of a road trip together, even though most of it will be flying."

"Yeah, that does sound like fun," said Ron. "I just need some time to process it. When is it? Can we talk after Christmas?"

"Of course, Ron," said Nathan in closing. "The trip doesn't start till spring break. But make sure you do call me in the new year—it will be fun. Give my best to Sara, now."

"Will do," said Ron. "Talk to you soon," as he hung up.

Nathan, thought Ron, already knowing that he wouldn't join him on his tour.

Ron had long since moved beyond jealousy, but Nathan Goldblatt had easily succeeded in nearly everything to which he'd aspired, whereas Ron's attempts at similar goals had meant struggle and had resulted in subpar results or even failure. He and Nathan, both English majors, had been roommates together at the UW and, along with Toby, had been fast friends—a nearly infamous trio in their year-class. Yet, despite the normal diversions and partying of undergraduates, Nathan had blossomed under the creative writing program and had earned top honors by the time he'd held his bachelor's degree. Ron, on the other hand, had seemed to perpetually suffer from writer's block when it counted most and had squeaked by, barely making the requirements needed to apply to grad school.

Ron remained surprised to this day that his friend was still a bachelor, as he was handsome, witty, and had been Sara's main squeeze, especially during their senior year. Sara had followed Nathan to the University of Chicago where Nathan had been accepted into the graduate English program, but she had become overwhelmed by both the size of the city and by the demands of the nursing school in which she'd enrolled, and had only lasted a single semester. The pair had split up amicably, but Ron had always wondered at Sara's apparent indifference to both the breakup and towards Nathan afterward.

Nathan had gone on to earn a PhD from Chicago, had gained a position as a professor of English at the University of Minnesota in Minneapolis, and on top of all that, he had become a prolific poet in his own right. Ron felt like a bum in comparison, but at least he had Sara. At least he hoped he did.

He resumed sorting through his own catalog of poems, but somehow with a more self-critical eye after his conversation with his friend.

<u>Eagle</u>

Ten pounds drooping the bough
Talons grip tight, twisting under each gust.
The battering storm
Leaves the bark scraped and torn.
But sudden clearing—
Wings unfold, outstretch
To a lift now weightless.
The branch tries to spring back.
Am I now as stooped and scarred
As was my father?

Ron had learned from his uncle a few years before he'd written this piece, that Paul and his brother, Frank, had been physically abused by their alcoholic father, and that Frank, being the eldest, had taken the brunt of it. This knowledge had put his father's parental palsy into perspective, and Ron had finally come to see that his father had not been acting out of hatred against him with his sternness and reproaches, but had been trying his best to cage and control any of the horrible examples of fatherhood that had been literally beaten into him when he was a child of Ron's age.

A meowing Cocoa had jumped up into his lap while he worked, and he carried the purring cat into the kitchen, setting him down beside his notice-how-empty-it-is bowl that Ron saw as half full. He refilled/topped it off with kibbles, depending on one's perspective, and then made himself a tomato and mozzarella sandwich from the ends of a sourdough bread loaf while enjoying a glass of chardonnay as a nice accompaniment. Sitting in the quiet kitchen while he ate, he took in the silence with a strange bite of loneliness. Usually, he loved his time to himself, but he somehow felt Sara's absence more acutely this evening.

Chapter 12.

By the time he was back at his computer, there had been several responses to his most recent post.

MargieP: Lovely poems. What will the title of your book be? I will look for it.

BL: How about Birds on the Brain for a title?

The blog had then devolved into a smattering of puns vying for the best name, the most recent of which he thought wasn't half bad.

BL: Or how about Birdgeoning Desires?

Ron ignored the suggestions that came after and considered posting one from among many of his brilliant insights into the publishing process that he'd drafted a month previously. But he thought he'd better read it through again first.

Who wouldn't like a little bit of monetary success in their new writing career? Unfortunately, it is not the author who is usually on the plus side of the pecuniary scale. We are not the harvesters—we are the harvest. I would wager that there is more money to be made by those who support authors than there is in authorship itself. If you are just getting started in the game, you would be amazed to learn of the number of businesses that are set up to help you along the way—for a cost, that is. Copy editing, editorial assessments, developmental editing, beta readers, cover design, interior design, self-publishing aids, marketing sites, advertising opportunities, prize contests, review providers... and on it goes. Many of these services are absolute essentials to even the most experienced authors, but many promise you the moon and never surpass the lower stratosphere brushing just above your launching pad.

Once you take up writing, you want to become the best you can be. At first you are striving to be somewhere near the top, maybe a bestseller, but then you eventually realize that settling for your personal best just has to be good enough. And that level of perfection is defined by your own innate abilities. You can only be so insightful, so distinct a voice, and come so close to a perfect story arc, no matter what the tools at your disposal. And this will vary from novel to novel.

But succeed you must. And there is an entire industry that has evolved around your desire to improve. Writing lessons will fix this, but we still need to work on that. This approach will give you the voice or character development that you're striving for. These online tools will help you hone your craft. These sites are designed for your specific marketing strategy and will add dozens of sales to your book... all for a price.

We may seem like we're living in better times than when a scribe runs down a muddy lane in the pouring rain with the single copy of a manuscript in his clutches, only to slip in pig slop and scatter the lot across a messy puddle. We may seem like we are, but trust me, we're not. Our pages get tossed into the dank sticky threads of the world-wide web, where they lie, sadly, soggily, stuck.

Ron spun around, pushed himself up from his seat, and headed for the kitchen and another glass of wine. Walking back into the study, he wondered if this last rant would depress his readers as much as it had depressed him. Trying to decide whether to post it, he sank back in his chair and found himself studying what he could make out of his own reflection in the dark window behind his computer screen. He saw that he looked angry. That this was probably the face that Sara encountered more frequently than not lately. He tried to relax his shoulders and facial muscles, but couldn't discern much difference in the reflection—which puzzled him since he felt a little depressed, maybe, but that was all.

He was about to message Sara at work to ask how she was doing but knew that she probably wouldn't have the chance to read it or respond. *I've been pushing her away,* he thought. And this brought the vision of her getting fed up and leaving for a life without him. Sara calling it quits because he drove her nuts. *Life without Sara...* he realized that he could conceive of this theoretically, but had to discount the notion out of hand because he believed that deep down she had come to live with and accept what he saw as mere idiosyncrasies and a rebel streak in himself. *After all—I have a real job, don't I? Why would she be unhappy, just because I go through phases?*

And if I'm unhappy sometimes, why is that? It's because the fucking decks are stacked against me, that's why! he fumed. *Stacked against almost all of us!* He was working himself up again, but for a good reason, he felt.

Then he recalled his earlier conversation with Sara and realized that she saw him as someone who was starting to be taken over by his own negative emotions, whereas he saw himself as a normal guy dealing with the challenges of being a player in an unfair game. Try as he might, however, rather than continuing to think about the effect the game was having on him, Ron instead drifted into dwelling again on the injustice itself. He suddenly pulled back up to his keyboard and began typing a follow-up piece about a pet peeve of his. There was a sense of satisfaction when he'd finished, but knowing better than to immediately post something he'd written in anger and haste, he shelved it for the time being.

OK, thought Ron, once he'd gotten that off his chest. *One more bird poem and then I'd better go pack.*

> In most of my past lives I have been a songbird.
> Not a far-sighted raptor piercingly hovering on
>   heights,
> Nor a patient heron, a still and silent reed.
> Not a pleasant duck rafting luscious lakes.
> No, I keep my head down, flitting for each single
>   seed.
> Ignorant of the vaster purpose in the quick heartbeat
>   of a little life.

He checked back for comments on his verses, but the discussion about potential book titles and ensuing puns continued. Not a single response to any of the poems, except for the initial one by MargieP. *Why do I even bother? I put out all this effort and get virtually nothing of any substance in return. It all just washes away. I get absolutely no recognition.* He sighed in mild frustration as he put the computer to sleep and headed upstairs to gather a small pile of clothes for the laundry.

As he started the washing machine and tried to organize for packing, he began to brood about just why he did bother to write and was soon back in the frame of mind to which he'd recently gravitated—convinced that he should stop writing altogether. By the time the laundry had finished, he was feeling dismal, not helped at all by a third glass of wine. Despite his decision to lay down his pen once and for all, he couldn't stop, and in his head he composed what he thought might be a fitting farewell poem.

But the words didn't just tumble out. He wandered over to a window as he tried to connect them and lifted the blind to gaze up at the thin clouds racing past the bright but waning moon. Ron had the image he was trying to describe vaguely in mind, but he'd also had enough wine that other thoughts flew past like those wispy clouds and grabbed his attention as they went by. *I'm mulling my words,* he thought, simultaneously rolling these words over his tongue as if he were speaking them. *Mulling,* he thought again. *Yeah, that's it. I mull my poems. Basically, I take a cheapo bottle of red wine, try and spice it up to hide how rotten it is, add some orange to try and make it relatable, and then I heat it up which is the opposite of what I would do if the wine was any good to start with. And then I serve it up for consumption, assuming that everyone else is freezing too, and would drink absolutely any warm beverage on a cold night.*

He found a spiral binder next to his bed and, scratching out several iterations, finally had a version that he felt he could post. It pretty much captured what he was feeling about the current state of his efforts.

<u>Inertia</u>

I'm mired in earth,
Ages since hewn by a hacker.
A bogged mirthless stump–
Its once singing roots
Now grounded unsheathed wires.
The fruit-filled exchange
With an energized sun
Is here and forever undone.

Ron glanced at the clock as he set down the notebook. *Ten-thirty. And Sara won't be home until after eleven. The perfect time for my little ritual.*

Chapter 13.

IT WAS the wrong lake, but there was a connection, nonetheless. And that made it good enough for Ron. The diminutive Yahara River linked the two bodies of water which meant that they shared the same cold fluids. Their surfaces were both frozen solid now so there was little to distinguish them from each other, or from the narrow isthmus that separated them, but it was their depths and commingling that mattered to him.

Ron was out on the ice of Lake Mendota to perform his semi-annual Rite of Rejection, and he always chose the clearest, windiest nights, making this a perfect evening for his task. The gusts were from the west, so he'd ridden a bus upwind to the University of Wisconsin campus, walking the few remaining blocks from the bus stand to the German-themed Rathskeller in the Student Union Building where he'd enjoyed a draft beer while rereading the five rejection letters he'd collected over the past few months. As opposed to the physical letters he'd received when he'd first begun submitting to publications, these recent replies had all arrived by email. However, since he felt that he needed paper to keep his tradition alive, he'd printed them out ahead of time and had stuffed them into an inner pocket of his parka. His therapist had also stressed that tangible paper was essential toward the effectiveness of the rite.

Four of the five he'd brought with him were form letters, so there was nothing special about them, but he'd reread them anyway. Each was slightly different in approach and verbiage, but all contained the same basic message. Thank you, but no thank you.

He'd lingered over the fifth letter—one he'd placed next to the others on the well-worn wooden tabletop as he'd finished his beer. It seemed to have been written by a real person who had actually read and considered his submission.

Dear Ron,

I quite enjoyed reading your poetry submission, Blankets, *but afterward I found myself in a quandary. The three sections were each good in their own right, although not solid enough to stand on their own, and yet, since no single section seemed to tie in with the others, I cannot accept the poem as a whole either.*

I would welcome a version that is more cohesive across its parts, or a fleshed-out version of one or more of the sections as a poem in itself.

Your work is promising, and please feel free to resubmit a revised copy at any time.

Sincerely,

Stanley Smith, Floating Cloud Press

Well, Ron had thought, *at least Stanley read it.* In response to Smith's comments, he'd attempted to rework *Blankets,* and had tried his best to link the three sections together without much success. The problem was that he'd intentionally meant for the poem to be disjointed, just like the layers of blankets on a bed. *Maybe I should have titled it* Comforter *instead of* Blankets, *he'd mused. But the poem as a whole is meant to show the layers of a personality we adopt as protections agains the cold world, and yet the image of a comforter stuffs them all together. It just doesn't work.*

He'd refolded the letters and tucked them away for his trip outside. The transition from the warm, steamy

Rathskeller into the wind-whipped bitter cold on the outdoor terrace had made him feel as if he'd momentarily blacked out, but Ron had adapted by the time his feet hit the lake ice.

As he now eased into a comfortably quick pace, he thought about an online essay he'd read by Jeff Shotts of the Graywolf Press. In *Jeff Shotts on the Art of Rejection*, he'd gained some insight into the mind of the editor-as-rejector, and it had tempered his reactions to the subsequent dismissals he'd received. Several lines of the essay had seemed especially pertinent when he'd read them.

The first thing to be said is: by practicing this art, you will disappoint, can only disappoint, you will always always disappoint. Your most practiced rejection, however worded, however encouraging you fashion it to be, is still a rejection. It is still a disappointment.

The next thing to say is: the editor must disappoint. Practice this art long enough, and you will disappoint many. Hundreds, and then thousands. You will carry this with you. You will lament that you have to hone a skill that makes you detestable.

You will always have rejected many, many, numerous many more than you can possibly ever accept. You will hope that you will be thought of, if you are thought of, as the editor who accepted the work of this author, and this author, and this author too. But you know, in truth, that the odds are every bit as stacked against you as they are for writers. You may more likely be known, if you are known, as the editor who rejected the work of this author, and this author, and this author too. – Jeff Shotts

While treking farther from the snowy shore, he recalled the depressing statistic Mr. Shotts had quoted which was that only 0.3% of submissions were accepted for publication at his agency.

At about the same time that he'd read this essay, Ron had become curious about the variety, yet sameness, of the rejections he'd received. He'd spent a day surfing on the topic of rejection letters and found hundreds of examples posted on the web. The most popular were, naturally, copies of letters received by famous authors and poets through the years—Wells, Orwell, Kipling, Vonnegut, Plath—they'd all received them, and the list went on. He had also discovered that there was an entire wiki site, *rejectionswiki.com,* that provided a surprisingly long list of boilerplate rejections indexed by magazine and publisher, along with copies of the various form letters the unlucky author submitting to them might receive. All of this had made Ron feel more closely related to the anonymous millions of rejected writers, whereas before this research he'd imagined himself as really belonging to the published family from which he'd somehow mistakenly been separated at birth.

Two iceboats off in the distance were taking advantage of the strong winds and the bright light of the nearly full moon to race each other, and apart from them and some dark figures that he could just make out walking much closer to the shoreline, he was alone on the mainly snow-free expanse of frozen Lake Mendota. Despite the radiant moonlight, the constellation Orion was still clearly visible, and down near the horizon flashed its constant companion Sirius, the Dog Star. His destination was Tenney Park, a public access spot where he could step off the lake fairly near his house, and the wind pushing behind him made him feel that it was urging him to hurry there, whereas he was really in no particular rush at all. Scattered patches of snow crunched under his feet when he reached them, and the crusted bits he dislodged flew away in dissolving pinwheels to join the faint hiss of icy particles that streamed ever east.

His father had left him when Ron was fourteen. While Ron was spending the day with a classmate, Frank had headed out on a Sunday drive to visit his brother, Paul, in La Crosse and had never come back. He'd abandoned Ron to fend for himself in the wilds of Wisconsin. The fact that it was an accident involving his father's car and an oncoming semi, and that they lived in the heart of Madison, never seemed to matter when his mood began to drop as the night's temperature had. The unfortunate thing had been the timing. He knew now that all relationships have their ups and downs, but unfortunately that with his father had been, to him, at a serious ebb. The two of them had fought constantly that year, and nothing Ron had done had been right or good enough. Ron had rebelled and his father had entrenched.

He wasn't even aware that Otis Redding had existed until that year. He'd discovered Otis among his uncle's records, and had spent many a night in a dark room listening to him and some selected blues artists who matched his sadness. He'd missed the sixties by a few decades, but by the time he'd turned seventeen he'd come to join the legions of fans who mourned the loss of an incredible talent, drowned in the depths of Lake Monona, Mendota's conjoined sister lake. He was nineteen when he'd received the first letter informing him that his submission of poetry to the New England Review was not quite up to snuff. He'd been listening to Otis as he'd read it, and somehow it had seemed a fitting tribute to sorrow to commit the letter to the same fate as the soulful singer. Only it had been winter at the time. And he lived nearer to Lake Mendota. Thus, the tradition.

Never content with being forced into a thick solid, the ice let out booms, pings, and eerie elongated moans as it settled, still protesting, into the heart of winter. Ron remembered racing across it as it did so. His father had taken him out on his iceboat several times when he was a child. He had wondered at it: the low sear of the boat's three skates as they tore across the ice; the stilling of the wind as they caught up with and then matched its speed; the feeling that they were sitting still while the lake sped by underneath them; the awe as they tacked at times on only two blades. Then he had become too big and too... something, for such trips. As was common between children and parents, he never found out what that second thing was.

Halfway to Tenney Park, he stopped. The wind was having none of this and pushed in fits for him to keep moving. In compliance, a thin cloud of his breath continued along this intended course, but the wind was not appeased in the slightest. Ron solemnly, but quickly, removed both of his mittens and placed them between his knees, squeezing tight. Then he unzipped his jacket and extracted the sheets of paper, immediately rezipping with his free hand. Both hands were now freezing, but he patiently took the pages and systematically tore them into the smallest bits he could manage, holding onto as many of the fragments as he was able. It was too cold for ceremony, but he took a moment of thought for all of those who had their talent cut short, or cut off even the slightest, pulled back the scraps in his right fist, and then threw them with the wind as hard as he could.

He usually enjoyed watching the flecks leap and race away, skittering against the hard surface, but that pleasure was denied him on this attempt. The gloves between his knees had meant his balance was off for this type of throw, and the transition from the backward movement into the forward motion of his arm had broken the truce between the soles of his boots and the ice. He was on his back before he could react, and his head made a convincing smack when it made contact with the dream of iceboats.

Part II
An Unexpected Will

Chapter 14.

RON REMEMBERED the slip, but not the landing. He couldn't get his eyes to open, and he wondered why the wind seemed to have stopped abruptly. He didn't think he'd passed out, and yet felt like he was just waking when he suddenly heard himself say, "Oooh," in a deeper and more guttural tone than he knew he was capable of.

To his surprise, he was no longer on his back, but in an awkward position—face down with his feet elevated on some object. *But, I fell backwards...* flitted briefly through his mind. A quick mental inventory and small jolts of pain told him that he wasn't paralyzed or had any life-threatening injuries. Finally, he got his eyes to open, but focusing them was another matter—only managing a blurred image with an odd lighting effect. He squeezed both eyes shut again and became aware of what felt like a cold draft hitting his left cheek—which was seemingly glued to the surface. *How odd,* he thought. *Must have numbed part of my face when I landed on the ice. It's gonna hurt even more when that wears off.*

With a groan, he pulled his feet down, managing to get himself into a position on all fours and then waited for a bout of ensuing nausea to pass. *And I must have numbed my brain, too,* he admitted as he began to regret the beer he'd drunk and tried to shake his head to clear it. Oddly enough, his body didn't respond, and he chalked it up to the fact that he might have strained his neck in the fall. He was aware enough, however, to register that he was no longer out on the lake, but inside a room—the unlikelihood of which momentarily tripped an internal mental circuit breaker—no thoughts were going anywhere. His vision had finally cleared, and he found himself staring down at a well-worn wooden floor, now stained with a few drops of what he took to be his own blood. But he didn't recognize this flooring. If he were at home, it should be the click-lock bamboo that he himself had installed the winter before. Now his hands, which were splayed out to support him, were registering the same cold his face had felt, rising from wide cracks between the unfamiliar planks.

I definitely must have hit pretty hard, he thought as he rocked back on his haunches and then sat on the bottom step of a flight of stairs—as if he knew they were there all along—and became concerned about the blood he'd seen. Both his head and jaw ached, and his nose felt like it had been punched—hard. He found himself patting his face for signs of damage, and his hands came back bloody. The red drops were evidently from a gash on the bridge of his nose and what must have been a large scrape along the left side of his forehead.

"Oh, you big clumsy oaf, you," came a deep voice. In shock, Ron tried to look around to see who had spoken, but was somehow unable to do so. Instead, he felt his mouth relax from speaking and a chuckle rumble from deep in his throat. This was especially odd, since Ron didn't feel the least bit amused at the moment. Instead, he felt a sense of dislocation that it was him—and yet not him—who had found this funny. *How strange,* he thought numbly, unable to pigeonhole what he was experiencing.

Then his attention was back to the floor and his immediate surroundings. *What the hell?* he wondered as his gaze raised and he tried to comprehend where he was and what he was seeing. The room was much smaller than his own living room, and as opposed to his six-panel front door at home, the one before him was comprised of stout wooden slabs with cross bracing, iron hardware, a secured peephole, and a black iron liftable latch. To the left was a tiny window paned in small glass diamond shapes held together with dark strips like the stained glass he'd seen at the Saturday Market on the streets that rounded Madison's capitol building.

Ron was startled when he involuntarily blinked hard several times and shook his head violently in what he took to be a much-delayed reaction to his previous attempt. He received a piercing pain in his head for the effort, and the unchanged scene began to trouble him. Experiencing an altered reality wasn't something entirely new to Ron, but those few times of experimentation had been exceedingly dreamlike and had never seemed so persistently real. This continuing hallucination might have been halfway expected if he had purposefully taken something to bring it on. Now he was suddenly worried about some brain damage due to the fall.

In fact, he was certain that he was still really laid out flat on the ice of Lake Mendota. He kept trying to elicit a vision of the night sky he knew should be before him, but all he saw was this small, unfamiliar room. He focused on feeling the cold and the wind that was surely buffeting him, but other than the draft coming up through the floorboards, the air remained calm. The thoughts he'd just had of his father and the emotions they evoked were still so present that a rough poem sprang to mind.

> Wind, snow hiss
> And Sirius.
> Alone on a frozen lake
> Under Orion,
> I fall into my father's footsteps.
> Not in the same place
> Given the nature of water and ice

But in a grudgingly similar space
With a familiar face
Following my father's missteps.
Wind, low hiss
And serious.
Alone on a frozen lake
Slipping and falling
Beneath an
Under-sympathetic sign.

I'll have to write that down, he thought. But, even this strong desire did nothing to jolt him out of his hallucination.

Still too shaken to stand, he noticed that the pain from his headache paled in comparison to that in his mouth. And to make matters worse, he also became aware of a persistent throbbing in his right foot until his mouth again grabbed his full attention. *Did I break a tooth when I fell?* Ron wondered. Without thinking, he dug his finger into his mouth and touched a tooth that sent his nerves into overdrive. An even bigger surprise to him though was that several of his teeth seemed to be missing. He pulled his finger back out and tried to study the floor for any small ivory-colored objects, but found himself unable to do so. There was no response—as if he'd lost control of his neck again. Then, unexpectedly to Ron anyway, he lifted his hand and examined it. Filthy fingernails, ground in grime, and a little finger that appeared to have been broken at some point, along with calluses thicker than he'd ever thought possible. There was a smear of wet blood on the finger that had touched the sensitive tooth. His forearms appeared to be massive, but he put this down to either visual perception or a dicey head injury. Then, realizing the foreignness of even his own hand, he mentally nodded to himself. *I'm having a doozy of a dream. That's the only explanation.*

And his foot was now begging for notice. Well-worn wool trousers led his eyes down to light boots or heavy socks made of a felted wool, and he removed one of these, pulling his right cuff up to reveal an angrily swollen ankle of bright pink. He made an exploratory rotation that made him yelp, but he found that he could move it up and down without it hurting as much, so walking would be painful but possible.

And that, he found out, was his next step. Ron replaced the boot, pushed himself up off the stairs, and was soon standing, but feeling oddly squat or stooped at the same time. He turned stiffly to look back at the stairs he'd apparently come down and found them to be half as wide and twice as steep as those that he knew in Madison. *What the hell is going on?* He wondered. *Time to call someone for a reality check,* as he attempted to reach into his pants pocket for his phone. Now it was his arms which seemed to be paralyzed and wouldn't respond to his commands. Yet somehow, they acted on their own now, dusting off his pants, feeling in the front pocket, and drawing out a thick ring with two attached skeleton keys. For some reason, he found himself nodding.

As if suddenly needing air, Ron headed for the door, lifted its latch, and threw it open. The unfamiliarity of the scene jolted him: crisp, morning air hit his face; the trees opposite the narrow road were just revealing a halo of green from new leaves; partially frosted mud showed the narrow tracks and hoof prints left by what must have been a passing cart; the lowing of a cow came from beside the house; and a middle-aged woman with a staff and a pile of what looked like raw wool on her back called across to him as she made her way along the opposite side of the road.

"Good morning to you, Mister Hart," she smiled with what Ron took to be a sudden glint in her eye. "May God be with you on this fine day."

In shock he found himself saying in a rough and low voice that he didn't recognize, "And to you Missus Jones, and to you," as he felt his heart beat faster and a small grin form on his mouth while giving a slight bow of his head and gently shutting the door.

Oh my God, he thought. *How did I know her name?* On top of that, he realized that what he had at first taken as pure gibberish had immediately made sense to him. He searched for any memory of her, but came up with a total blank.

Seeing Mrs. Jones had made him realize that he might not be alone in this house. Rather than creep about, he tried to bravely call out, "Hello?," and repeated the attempt several times with no corresponding movement of mouth nor larynx. *Am I dumb?* he wondered. *I just spoke to the woman outside though... And she called me Mr. Hart. Who the hell is that? I don't think I've ever had a dream where I was someone else...* Temporarily abandoning that train of thought, he then felt eager to explore this space that was apparently his own, or, if not, one in which he was expected. This room in which he'd planted his face was about twelve feet on each side and held a half-enclosed fire pit near the end away from the stairs, against an outer wall. Embers glowed in the center of the pit, and some smoke trailed up to an open vent in the roof above the short second story. The stairs led down from a loft that extended to the middle of the room and ran for what appeared to be the length of the house. The floor, he now noticed, was much better constructed than he had originally thought, and the gaps between boards were mostly filled with straw and mud to prevent leaks. The small window next to the door was the only glassed one in the house, and all the other framed openings were shuttered to keep out the morning cold. There was a bench and a stout table, several candles, and a sitting chair in the room. A worn felted wool rug was near the fire pit, and one wall had a cloth hanging of faded red and green. The walls were a timber frame construction with large posts, beams, and diagonal supports, filled between with compacted mud and straw. Most of the infill had been whitewashed at some point, but soot and grime had obviously long since dominated the surfaces.

To the left of the stairs he was facing was another smaller room that held a modest eating area, judging by the table and chair in its middle, and off of this appeared to be the kitchen with a cooking fire alcove located up against the opposite end of the house from the firepit. He wandered into that section, limping slightly as he did so. Again, there was no chimney per se, rather an open path for the smoke to reach the roof vent. A large iron pot hung above the cooking area ashes, some wooden bowls and platters lay about the tabletop, as well as various clay jars and jugs containing not much he could immediately identify. Woven garlic and bundles of dried plants hung from various black iron hooks, as did the remains of a mostly bone leg of something lamb sized. A small wheel of cheese sat on a rough highboy, along with two round loaves of a nearly-black bread. He opened a cabinet on an exterior wall and found another leg of lamb, a smoked ham, a crock of butter, another of lard, and some more cheese. He dipped his finger in the lard and rubbed it on the bridge of his nose, apparently to staunch the small trickle that still oozed from the wound.

There were several small kegs and a pitcher on the floor against the wall. He was suddenly parched and tried to look around for some water. There were no taps nor a well pump, but Ron expected there to be water somewhere in this kitchen, and glancing around he finally discovered some in a bucket. However, with some flies floating in it, its potability looked dubious. Against his will, he apparently decided to try it anyway, and picked up the bucket, catching a glimpse of his face reflected off the water's surface as he did so. *Ugh,* he thought. Split skin on his nose and a nasty gash on the forehead now both glistening with grease, unkempt, curly hair, thick nose and lips, and a bristly week-old beard showing touches of gray—this was definitely not his face. *What a dream!* he thought. *How do I make this stuff up?*

Rather than dipping a mug into the bucket to take a drink, he found himself pouring some into a nearby bowl. He took up a tattered rag, wet it in the water, and began dabbing the blood off his face.

He carried the bowl of now-pink water over to the corner of the kitchen and dumped it into a small ditch that ran under the wall to the outside of the house. Back at the table, he peeked in a pitcher and smelled the contents, finding it to be a stale beer of some sort. He filled a nearby mug and meaning to take an exploratory sip, took a healthy glug instead. It was pleasantly mild, spiced with something he couldn't identify, and looked clean enough, so he drained the mug. *Not bad,* he thought as he realized at the same moment that it wasn't him who'd made the conscious decision to move to this unusual, but safer, choice of drink.

Next, he headed upstairs, which was not something he'd considered doing at all. As with most of his actions so far, it was as if he were on autopilot. He climbed the narrow, steep staircase that was more like a ladder, and once at the top he was in the low-ceilinged loft. Open to the ground floor along its length, he wanted to stay away from the edge and, seemingly in accordance with this wish, moved inward and found several chests, a small table and stool, and a single short, low bed. *I must live alone,* he thought while taking in the sparse sleeping area. As stooped as his body seemed to be, he instinctively tried to duck even lower as he moved toward the bed that was situated closer to the eaves, but discovered that he still had inches to spare from the height he was accustomed to. In fact, after assessing himself and his belongings, he guessed that he could be a foot shorter than he had been in what seemed like moments before in Madison. The bed looked comfortable but visibly short, and he found himself adjusting his expectations to match his current stature. The chests had no locks, and opening each revealed nothing but a little clothing and additional bedding. He moved aside a quilt and reached for a thick wool sweater, donning it with a slightly sweet/rank smell of something familiar, but difficult to immediately pinpoint, rising with it as he did so.

Chapter 15.

RON HAD wondered where exactly this house was located and was curious about its surroundings. With the donning of the sweater, he guessed that he was about to find out. However, although further exploration might have been amusing, he was overcome by the desire to rouse himself out of this dream, not wanting to freeze to death on the ice in Madison. He tried to will himself awake, but instead it was like he was locked in someone else's footsteps, which now struck him as a real possibility.

When he reached the head of the stairs, Ron suddenly thought, *If I woke up here after I—this guy—fell down the stairs, maybe the way back to reality is to fall down them again.* With an effort, and feeling like he was rearing back, he then tried to lunge forward—in fact, he could almost feel his presence throwing itself into his—this Mister Hart's—chest to tip him over. But absolutely nothing happened. Mister Hart remained steady, and Ron was left stunned by his own ineffectiveness.

Rather than tumbling down, he descended the steep stairway in measured steps, annoyingly taking care as he did so. Once at the entry, he removed his felt boots, stepped into some laceless leather shoes, pulled open the front door, and turned to the right as soon as he was off the shaved log that served as a front stoop. Attached to the side of the house was another lower building with a wide barn-style door. He approached the door, grabbed a long wooden handle, and with a tug, slid it partway open. Before him lay a motley assortment of spoked wheels of all sizes and styles—a few with steel rims, some missing spokes, many with cracked hubs—along with the lumber and tools necessary to repair them. *If this is where I work—where he works—then I'd guess he's a wheel maker... a wheelwright,* he realized as he stepped into the workshop. He saw several familiar looking tools, but dominating the center toward the rear was a contraption he didn't immediately recognize. A sturdy post held a wooden arm that extended out above a workspace and from it a thick cord dropped down to a horizontal spindle and wrapped around it several times. He walked toward the device feeling perplexed about its use until he finally figured out what it might be—a lathe. But his body acted as if it knew this all along. He took up a sharp chisel from a nearby bench and held it ready against a support as his foot found the treadle that it sought. As he pushed down on the treadle, the horizontal piece of wood held between a pair of spindles began to spin toward him. When he let up his foot, it reversed direction as the overhead arm that had bowed down on the downstroke pulled back up on the cord as it returned to its resting state. And so, he spent some time at the lathe, cutting at the wood with the chisel on the down stroke and holding back on the upstroke. *Ah, I'm shaping a spoke for a wheel,* he realized, and finally noticed a completed example sitting on the bench beside him as confirmation.

Ron had been mesmerized by this entire experience, but then mentally stepped back. *OK, this clinches it. I know nothing about wheel making, and I could never have imagined this lathe contraption. I know nothing about this time period or this... England. They were speaking an old English. I think. This can't be a dream. But, then what else could it be?*

He was startled when there was a sudden shadow at the half-opened door, and the silhouette which cast it moved inside, pulling the door shut as it did so. Ron froze and, meaning to hold up the chisel in defense, was about to cry out when a voice said, "Hello again, Mister Hart." His brain couldn't compute what was happening, but he set the chisel down and was suddenly moving towards the roundish figure, feeling an unexpected grin spread across his face. He was soon wrapped up in the arms of Mrs. Jones, and he could taste the memory of a spiced meal on her lips, smell the reality of sour lanolin in her hair—the smell he now identified as matching that from his sweater. "What happened? A fall?" she asked as she pulled away from the embrace and gently touched his forehead, then leaned forward to kiss his nose. All he could think to do was nod in reply, but found himself saying, "That floor is harder than my head."

She smiled and backed him over to a cot in the corner covered by a straw-stuffed mat and, after some fiddling, Mrs. Jones' white breasts became visible in the dim light provided by the cracks in the wall planks. *What? Whoa! wait a sec...* thought Ron in surprise. With her skirt up and both of their drawers down, they fell onto the cot caressing, with soft sweet words coming from his companion. Ron registered a somehow pleasing spectrum of odors on and around them as their coupling began, and his head was spinning with the unexpectedness of it all. In the middle of their, 'humping' was the word that came to mind since he felt so disconnected from the experience, a realization came to him. *Ah,* he thought. *So, I guess this is all a dream after all. I'm having a sex dream. And I sure wouldn't betray Sara if it wasn't.* Then his next thought was, *I sure as hell hope Mrs. Jones isn't cheating on her husband with this Mister Hart.*

They'd held each other for a time afterward, and then when they were standing and rearranging things, Mrs. Jones asked, "So, Mister Hart, is the wheel for my spinner finished yet?" She had red apple cheeks, thin brown hair with a touch of gray, eyes to match, a dimple when she smiled, and horribly brown teeth. His mind panicked for a reply, but he found himself saying, with a smile on his face, "Not yet, Missus Jones. Not yet." Ron somehow knew that they had been saying this same thing for quite some time. She grabbed his hand and held it as they walked to the door. "Good," she said. He pulled the door open and noticed the bundle of wool which had been stashed to the side. He helped her secure her load and then watched her pick her way through the mud and ruts to her home. *Wherever that place might be and with whomever it was she shared it,* Ron wondered.

Rather than returning to the shop, Ron found himself sliding the door shut and plodding to the house in a daze, approaching the small bench at the table inside, and plopping himself down. It was an odd feeling for Ron—being mentally shaken but bodily at ease with what was happening. There was no hint of an adrenaline rush or jitters regardless of his inner thoughts. Yet there was something about this corporeal awareness that made him think that this might not be a dream after all. It certainly was nothing like the daydream of skating out on the ice of Lake Mendota with Joni Mitchell. He was troubled by this sense of detachment from his physical self and in response, tried to grip the bench and yell out "Wake up!" into the empty room, but oddly all that came out was a gigantic yawn. He tried another, more emphatic, "Wake up, Ron!" with no effect, only a follow-up stifled yawn. So, it was still questionable whether either of these attempted actions would have served to rouse him, as might pinching himself, say, if this was, in fact, a dream. Then to his great surprise, he reached up and slapped his own face, dully feeling the sting. *Nope, I don't think I'm dreaming,* thought Ron, vacillating on the subject once again, when out of the blue he said aloud, "Get going, John, you log, you."

John. He called me - or himself John. Then that means he's Mr. John Hart, whoever the hell that is. It definitely isn't me. Ron, who had just become acquainted with John, already wanted to be done with him. *Enough of this,* he thought, and he was positive that the only way to wake up out of this was to fall down the stairs once again. He tried with all his might to stand up and climb the staircase. He did eventually stand, but Ron found it impossible to will himself, or John, up those stairs. *John, go up the stairs,* he said, or rather, thought at the beginning. And, he had soon worked himself into a lather, mentally shouting, *God dammit, John! Go up the fucking stairs!*

There was absolutely no reaction. His physical body—John's, in fact—continued with what must be normal routine—sweeping detritus from the floors into the firepit, trimming the candle wicks, cutting some bread and cheese, and lighting a fire under the hanging stewpot.

No matter the level of his emotions, nor his attempts to move as he wanted or scream out loud, his body—John's body - didn't seem to care. Ron, on the other hand, was exhausted.

John had finished a light meal and was just wiping out his wooden bowl when he heard a gentle rapping on his door. He wiped his hands, walked to the entry, and lifted the latch.

"Hello, John," said a pleasant looking young woman in a clean linen dress.

"Martha," replied John warmly. "What brings you here?"

"I hope you are not busy. My mistress's husband has gone out to make final preparations for our trip to Henley today, and she thought she could steal some time for you. She says that everything is laid out and she's ready."

Oh, my God, thought Ron. *What is this John? The local Lothario?*

"Yes, Martha, I can come with you at once," as he stepped down onto the street with her.

Definitely a sex dream, thought Ron.

After exchanging pleasantries, John asked, "Do you think you and the mistress will be back in time for the wake?" while keeping to the muddier sections of the road in deference to Martha as they walked toward what Ron took to be the center of a small town. Ron found himself wondering who had died.

"Yes, yes, that is the plan. Back for the wake and then off to Kenilworth soon after that. I don't think I've travelled so much as I will in the next few days," said an excited Martha.

After passing a long row of thatched and whitewashed houses on the right, they came to some cross streets, and when John looked up, Ron noticed a church in the distance. They stopped before a two-story timber-frame house and Martha opened the door, requesting him to enter.

John stepped in and a well-dressed, very slight woman was sitting at a nearby desk. She nodded at them, and John said, "Hello, Mistress Jane."

"Greetings, John," the lady replied.

By the time John had slipped off his boots, Mistress Jane had arranged some papers and was dipping a quill in ink. "I'm glad that you could come on such short notice. We'd better get started, as I don't have much time before we depart." Two pieces of paper lay ready on the desk. *Oh, this is what she had laid out,* though Ron with an odd sense of relief.

"Now, remember we have talked about the letter 'a', and how it has its name sound, 'aee,'" she sounded out, "and its secret sound 'ah.'"

John, standing slightly behind her and on her writing side, nodded.

"So, we are at the letter 'e' which is a very interesting letter. It has its name sound of 'eee', as in the word 'she', and it has a secret sound of 'eh' as in pen." She wrote both words out for John. "We can work through more examples later, but I wanted you to know that it also has times when it is absolutely silent."

John paused for a moment and then asked, "Well, excuse me Mistress, but what use is that?"

"Oh, but it is useful indeed, John. Here, let me show you."

She redipped the quill, and then wrote out the word 'cap.' "Can you say this word?"

John took a moment and then slowly sounded out the word.

"See? The letter 'a' has its secret sound. But when I add the letter 'e' to the end of the word, it becomes the word 'cape,'" as she wrote the letter 'e' and sounded out the new word. "The 'e' stays quiet, but it makes the letter 'a' say its name sound." Mistress Jane then wrote out many examples, several of which John was successful in reading aloud.

In the meantime, Martha had been bustling about in preparation for the trip, and now brought out two hampers of provisions to position near the door.

A tolling church bell was made louder when a servant entered the house to take out the hampers. "I think I am out of time for our lesson, John, but I wanted to make sure you learned about the letter 'e' before I left."

John nodded and hastened over to put on his boots.

"Thank you, Mistress Jane. That was very helpful. Very helpful, indeed."

"You are so welcome, John. And thank you for watching over our house while we are away."

John wished her a safe journey before heading back in the direction of his house. He stopped in front of the shop, threw open the door, and walked over to rekindle a fire in the shop's firepit from wood shavings and scraps of wood to warm the space against the spring chill. He then settled into work.

❧

Ron was still thinking about the lesson. He realized that he took literacy so much for granted, that it was some time before the implications of this older man trying to learn to read began to sink in. *In all likelihood, very few here can read or write, and so that means that the ability to become a poet is probably vanishingly small,* and he would have shaken his head had he been able.

Two spokes were completed and a third well underway when there came a rapping on the plank door and a large gentleman poked his head in. "Is that Mister Hart?" he asked.

"Yes? Please enter," said John, seemingly unsure of to whom he was speaking.

"Simon Talbot," the speaker reminded him, "for Mister Penworthy?"

"Oh, yes, Simon, how are you?" asked John, with Ron more accustomed now to letting John's mouth take over from what he himself was really thinking.

"Very well, thank you. I'm inquiring about the Master's carriage wheel?"

"Yes, yes, Simon. I am forming the spokes as we speak. I still have six more to fashion, and then it will take a day or two to assemble the wheel. Say, three or four days more?"

"Very well," replied Simon. "I'll let the Master know. Getting about by foot is becoming vexing for him now, so he will be pleased to hear of it."

"Yes, I'm sorry to learn that his problem has returned. I will try and deliver the wheel soon."

Simon nodded and was about to set off when John called to him. "Oh, Simon?" The man turned back toward the shop. "Do you have anyone who can help me reset the wheel?"

"Yes, me and a couple of the lads should be able to manage it."

"Very well, see you then," said John, with Ron thinking, *Why did I say that? I have no idea where he lives or even where the hell I am right now.*

After Simon left, John walked over to a slate that was propped on a bench by the door and examined it. To Ron it initially made no sense at all. Poorly scratched letters, some written backwards, an 'f' where he thought an 's' should be. And then it suddenly became unscrambled and clear to him. Mister Hart was a poor speller and calligrapher, but the words were recognizable to him now. He saw that 'Pen' with a backward 'P' was written at the top for Penworthy, and the fmith that was the next down had morphed into Smith. The name Jones was scribbled at the bottom of the list.

John had begun to move away, but Ron could feel a smile on the man's face as he turned back to the slate. He took up a small fragment of chalk and then sketched a letter 'e' behind the letters 'drak', and proudly sounded out the name 'Drake'.

He then rubbed out the backwards 'P' in 'Pen' and corrected it with hesitant strokes. Stepping back to reexamine the slate, John scratched his chin and then shook his head. He rubbed out the corrected 'P' and wrote it backwards as it had been, finally satisfied with the spelling. *Bit of dyslexia, I'd say,* thought Ron.

By chance, there had been no 'f's for 's's in the words that Mistress Jane had written out, and as John walked back to the lathe to engage with another spoke, Ron confirmed that from everything he'd seen, and now from the use of old script on the slate tablet, that his current strange existence was set in an England of many centuries past. *Now, why would I choose to conjure up this place and time?* he wondered.

Ron made several attempts during the afternoon to stop work and investigate just where he was in England, but he couldn't will himself—his physical body—to leave the lathe and the work at hand.

He continued pondering his presence in this body of Mister John Hart while the man shaped the turning wood. *I wonder if he knows I'm here? I haven't seen any sign of it if he does. Of course, how would he react if he did? Grab his head and scream? Smash it against a stone wall? I know I would. What do I do if he starts thinking about me? I'm trapped here. I'm not able to move where I want or say what I want, but he can. Well, it is his existence, after all. I'm just a creepy alien mind-meld. This is just too weird. I wish I could snap my fingers...* And Ron spent several futile minutes trying to do just that while John turned the lathe.

Chapter 16.

THE SUN was near setting when he put down the chisel, arranged the completed spokes, checked that the fire was almost out, and opened the door onto the muddy street. Then, unexpectedly, to Ron anyway, he turned back into the shop, filled a wooden bucket with the chips from his work on the lathe, and scattered them on the road in front of his workshop. Then, replacing the bucket, he closed up, stepped out onto the chips and headed in the opposite direction from the house for, as Ron was to soon discover, the local tavern.

His, John's, home was located near the end of a lane along a row of houses, most larger than his, and situated across from newly harrowed fields somewhat obscured by a windbreak of trees. After passing a few houses on his right, a large stone church became apparent on a small rise to the left. A smattering of gravestones at its base cast their long shadows in the last of the sun's rays. The street was active with women pulling laundry off bushes and lines, children shooing chickens in through gates, and sheep and cows being herded into enclosures. Ron said hello or nodded to many as he passed, and there were many happy returns.

The tavern was located on what Ron estimated to be a long city block from the church in a ramshackle building which featured a bell hanging from an iron arm fastened out front. Ron mentally braced himself as he entered, not knowing what to expect but with visions of either rowdy men and bawdy women or of mean stares with pistols and knives on display. The interior scene was neither of these. There was a fire burning at one end of the compact space and small tables and benches were scattered about. A few of the patrons seemed to know him, and he patted one man heartily on the shoulder as he passed by.

John reached into his pocket and withdrew a coin in exchange for a tankard of whatever came out of the keg. Taking a hearty gulp, it proved to be a strong ale. "Thanks, William," he said as he braced his elbows on the small counter between him and the tavern keeper.

"You're most welcome, John," said William, leaning in closer to examine his customer's face. "Hit your head with a hammer again, did you? Or have a run-in with those Webb brothers?"

He laughed and touched his forehead. "Nah, took a tumble down the stairs this morning." He paused and then added, "And, I had none of your pints yesterday!"

Several of those within earshot chuckled and one shouted, "None too many!" Bringing more laughter.

"Don't fall down too often there, John," said William. "I need your business." He then launched into what Ron guessed was a familiar telling of his plans to tear down this old shack and build a proper tavern in its place as soon as he had enough capital.

Despite the sales pitch, John appeared to stick to just a single tankard, gravitating over to a seat near the fire and spending most of his time sipping and staring into the flames.

Ron, unsurprisingly, felt himself becoming—not bored, but, *unstimulated*, he finally decided on the proper descriptor. And he knew why. Were he in a tavern at home, he'd be chatting with a friend, checking his phone, listening to music, and glancing at the multiple TV screens. Here, there was nothing . Nothing but a crackling fire and low conversations in the background.

One of the men who had overheard John's earlier conversation came over and laid a hand on John's back. "Are you feeling alright, John?" he asked. "I heard about your tumble."

"Yes, Jacob, I'm fine. Just feeling the day is all." Which left Ron wondering if what John was really feeling was a little bit of Ron inside his head.

Afterward, John walked home in the gathering dusk, cooked a thin lamb stew, tidied up and went to bed, falling asleep as soon as his head hit the pillow.

Whew, what a day—what a dream I've been having, thought Ron, having wondered if he would be asleep at the same moment as John. *Now all I have to do is drift off, and hopefully I'll wake up back on the ice in Madison.* The thought came with a great sense of relief. However, sleep didn't come easily.

Ron had heard of lucid dreaming and astral projection and spent a long time trying to focus his mind, envisioning himself levitating out of John's body and floating back to Lake Mendota. He remained, however, just as John was— inert. Still, he was convinced that his reality was in the twenty-first century, and that this was only a temporary phantasm.

As it happened, this conviction proved to be insufficiently strong to keep his thoughts from running away with themselves. Ron soon became frantic over the possibilities about what might have happened to himself in Madison: he was dead, frozen stiff on the ice; he'd had a serious aneurysm; he'd stepped into another dimension; this was all a persistent dream and he really lay on a hospital bed in a coma. *Or, I've stepped into someone else's life and have inhabited the poor bastard,* was his final thought along these lines. And he concluded that the last scenario might just be the case.

Another jolt of panic hit him as he wondered what had happened to others since he was no longer in Madison, or even the twenty-first century, for that matter. He was apoplectic for a moment, realizing what his disappearance would do to Sara after she shifted from fury to worry when she realized that he was not coming home. Then followed fretting about Crone Amplifiers without him holding up his end. Silly thoughts beset him like the overdue gas bill, tomorrow's garbage collection, the cat box that Sara never changed, taxes which he always took care of. His uncle, his friends, his blog. His blog. It occurred to him that he'd considered this last, while prior to this 'incident,' as he now thought of it, the blog had been his highest priority. And his poetry. Why wasn't he concerned about his poetry and the now actualized possibility that he would never write again? Had he so internalized his decision to quit?

Calming himself, it was his change in time period more than in space that dominated his thoughts. *No electricity, no cars, no planes, no instant communications, very little glass, no zippers let alone Velcro, few books, no photographs, no antibiotics... This experience will be something to write about when I get back.* He was struck by the spareness of everything he had seen. He'd caught a glimpse of a meager bookshelf against a wall and two books on Mistress Jane's desk. One book, which appeared to be a bible, had been bound in leather and the other appeared to have a wooden cover. *What a contrast to our multitudes of paperbacks and our loud book covers,* he thought.

Beginning to tire and in the dark and quiet, he felt that he was back in Madison, tucked into his own bed. As if out of habit, he had soon formulated another rant for his blog just before he drifted off to sleep. This one prompted by those two unadorned books.

Like being in a crowded room where, as the conversations progress, everyone is shouting to be heard, our book covers are now screeching. Bold titles with neon blocky shapes fighting to grab the reader's attention yet, in a way, they all now look the same.

Book covers present another marketing mystery, especially to self-publishing authors. Besides being told that a superior title and blurb at the back are absolutely essential to making a book stand out from the rest, we are also told that an outstanding book cover will make the sale. So, if the book is ignored, was it the font selection? The color combination? The cover art? The blurb at the back? What the hell was it??

Anyway, book covers are never easy, but they may be easiest for poets. Unless there is an underlying theme to the collection, a cover only needs to look artistic (says the non-artist.) A display solely of words arranged uniquely in an interesting font; a sketch of a bird just alighting on a branch; a black and white photo of cherry blossoms with a single petal colored in pink; a rain-soaked alley with the reflection of a neon sign in a puddle. You get the drift, the sky's the limit because it only needs to convey atmosphere. To oversimplify, covers are also easier for non-fiction books since the cover should be about the subject matter. Woodworking? Better show some wood or tools.

Fiction is another matter, however, and it can't be easy to stand out these days in romance, mystery, and science fiction. I have sympathy for fiction writers. How many new ways are there to show a hunky man and a lustful woman in an interesting way? To entice a reader into an urban murder (oh, yeah, the cover of a rain-soaked alley with the reflection of a neon sign would also work here?) To portray an alien world with strange plants and three moons that isn't a copy of all the others?

Cover art is difficult, but it really shouldn't matter if the writing is good. Right? Has anyone seen the original covers of Ulysses *by Joyce?* City *by Simak?* The Big Sleep *by Hammett?*

We're all just ordinary people, but you might not know it by the picture of the author on the back. If you write a western, you gotta have a cowboy hat or something with a horse, a cabin, woods, or vast rangeland in the background. If a poet—black and white, books or bookshelf in the background, without a smile and facing the camera. Mystery writer—surprisingly similar to a poet, but it works to add a gun, some smoke, or fog.

We're part of the marketing expectations—if you want to sell something you must look the part, and it will never be how you look in real life. You'll never see a book jacket picture of a romance novelist on a picnic with her husband and kids; never see a mystery writer sampling cheese at a delicatessen; never see a sci-fi writer standing in line at the supermarket checkout. C.J. Box in shorts at the beach? Not gonna happen.

Ron felt totally at home as he fell asleep, already looking forward to seeing Sara when he came to.

Chapter 17.

BIRD SONGS and the first light of day woke them both. In Ron's case, it was with a visual poem in his head inspired by the distinctive call of a cuckoo he'd heard for the first time the day before—a poem that hit remarkably close to the truth.

One, two,
- oh damn   I lost count
One, two,   *What lies outside*   three, four.
Four? How could   *this shell? When will they*   it be four?
Was I asleep   *notice I don't fit?*   when I laid
that last   one? I'm
losing my mind.

His heart sank when he realized that he was still in a little house somewhere in England. *I've never fallen asleep in a dream, only to wake up in the same dream,* he thought. *I wonder if anyone has?*

John, on the other hand, was humming and scratched again at a place that had been bedeviling him all night. He sat up, stretched, and then pulled on trousers, a linen shirt, and what Ron took to be a woolen tunic or coat, securing it with a sash. He slid on his felted boots and moved to the stairs.

Ron was suddenly wide awake and energized. *Now's my chance!* As John took his first cautious step down the stairway, Ron envisioned himself collapsing and throwing the entire weight of his being into John's knees to send the poor man crashing down the remaining steps. *Well, it was worth a try,* he ventured while John easily navigated the remainder on his way to the lower floor.

Once down, Ron found himself unexpectedly intent on finding a pen and paper to record his poem even though he knew the likelihood of being able to use them was slim to none. It was then that he realized there were times when he and John were in sync, as John began searching the house for something as well. Ron found nothing, but John had opened a wooden box containing some chalk to replenish that used on the slate in his shop.

He rekindled the fire in the kitchen, set some water to boil, and made a thin porridge with a handful of acorns thrown in. Ron had never eaten acorns, and enjoyed the breakfast, although he might have roasted the nuts first and added some salt and pepper if asked.

Then it was into the shop to assemble Mister Penworthy's wheel. John muttered something under his breath as he began, but even Ron, being as close to John as anyone was likely to get, couldn't make out what he'd said. He hoisted a wheel hub that he'd already fashioned up onto a waist-high stand, and then began to chisel out every roughly formed mortise in turn to make a perfect fit before driving each spoke home with a wooden mallet. He'd completed four of the ten by mid-morning when there was a gentle knock on the door.

Ron expected to see Mrs. Jones' smiling face as the door opened, but the silhouette was much shorter and thinner on this occasion. "Master Will!" said John as he set his mallet on the workbench and approached the lad who Ron took to be about 10 years of age. "What brings you to Welford on such a fine morning?" *Welford, England!* thought Ron at the same moment. And then, *I have no idea where that is—I'll have to look it up on a map. If I can find one.*

"Good morning, Mister Hart," said the boy. "I came to see my Aunt Jane, but no one answers in the house. Is she away?"

"Yes, lad, she and her husband have gone to Henley to take care of some business. They will be back here for a night or two, but then plan on traveling to Kenilworth to make ready for the renewed Hocktide celebration next week and to see the very Queen herself," said John as Ron was thinking, *Wow, that is the longest string of words I've heard yet from this man.*

"Yes!" exclaimed Will. "Father says that we may go as well! The Queen! Are you going, Mister Hart?"

"Alas, but such are for younger, more well-to-do folks, I think."

"But have you ever been to Kenilworth? Have you ever seen the Queen?"

"No, and I don't expect to, neither. I will have a time come upon me when I can work no longer, so I'm going to make use of the time that I have yet to put chisel to wood."

Ron uselessly screamed, *Go see the frigging Queen! You bloody idiot!* realizing that the queen during this period had to be either Mary or Elizabeth. The chance of a lifetime. *And I wouldn't mind seeing her myself... but, 'bloody idiot'?* This British thing was starting to seep into him.

Will nodded and then said, a little less enthusiastically, "Yes, but even so, it is the Queen."

"I know, Master Will. But this will give you a chance to tell me stories of it when you return."

"Oh, I shall!" grinned Will, but the grin quickly faded.

"What is it young Master?"

"It is nothing really, but Auntie promised to show me some poems before she left. One, she said she wrote herself. And now she's already departed north."

A poet? wondered Ron. *Maybe they're not as rare here as I thought.*

"Well, now, I don't know anything about poesy, but Mistress Jane did leave me the keys to her home and entrusted me to look in on it now and then. What do you say we go over and see if she left something for you?"

Ah, the woman John had lessons with, thought Ron.

"Yes, please!" replied Will with a renewed smile as John turned and checked on the progress he'd made on the wheel thus far, made sure the small fire was secure, and then led the boy out into the bright day.

"But first, let's get you a bite to eat."

John led the way to his house after closing the shop door behind them. "And, so how did you get here, Master Will? Not walk all this way, I hope?"

"No, I started off walking, but then the apothecary, Mister Willis, gave me a ride. He was going on to Bidford, but set me down at the bridge."

"Ah, Mister Willis," nodded John in reply. "He saw to my Mary."

Will's expression suddenly sagged and he nodded without responding.

Ron guessed that something had happened to John's Mary, but had no way of asking about it.

John laid out an easy early lunch, really all he had available, of cheese, bread, and a cup of milk. The boy wolfed his portion down and caught John up on his new baby brother, Richard, and his younger brother and sisters, Gilbert, Anne, and Joan.

"That is so good to hear, Will, that all is well with your family," said John and then told Will about the latest news of the Hart clan, ending with, "And your school is going well?"

Will replied with a string of Latin that must have been gibberish to John, too, because Ron didn't understand a word, and John was shaking his head at the end. "Well, now that is quite like the priest used to say at mass when I was but a little tyke," he said.

Will merely nodded his head. Ron remembered something about the conflict between the new Church of England and the Catholic Church around this time and guessed that Will felt it best not to ask much about religion or papistry of anyone.

"I thought the Latin was for nothing at first, but there come to be many fine things written in it," said Will.

"As I've heard," said John, nodding in reply. "As I've heard."

He swept the crumbs from the table into his hand, picking up the remaining crusts as well, and asked, "Are you sated? Would you like some more?"

"No, thank you, Mister Hart, it was a very fine meal."

"Well then, let's us go and see what Mistress Jane has left for you."

The wind hit them as they set out along the lane, and Will thrust his hands into his pockets. A few houses down, John paused to throw the crumbs and the stale bread he'd brought to a flock of chickens being watched over by a young girl. "There you go, Alice," he said with a grin. "You mind those chicks now, you hear?"

"Yes, sir, Mister Hart," said the girl, taking her time to enunciate the words distinctly, as if rehearsing for a part in a play. She then grinned and ran up and hugged his leg while he patted her head.

"Well done, Alice, well done," said John.

They had moved further up the road when John said, "She's had a tough go with no father, and didn't talk until just this spring. We're all glad that she's come around."

Will turned and walked backwards for several paces watching her feed the chickens. "What would it be like to never talk?" he asked as he turned back around.

Hey, I know something about that! shouted Ron, but John gave no response. *So strange,* thought Ron. *I can almost feel my mouth and vocal cords working as I say things, but nothing comes out.*

They reached the now-familiar large two-story thatched house a block back from the church, when John walked up to the door and fit one of the two black skeleton keys into the lock.

The wind blew in with them and scattered some oak leaves across the floor. As Ron now knew, the space inside was several giant steps up from John's home in both size and furnishings. Brick fireplaces with chimneys rose up each end of the house, glass oil lamps were on the polished tables, small painted portraits hung on the walls, a case held several books accompanied by a reading stand to the side, upholstered chairs and some stuffed pillows were arranged near the fire. *And the paper, ink, and quill pens at that writing desk!* exclaimed Ron to himself. *Let's go over there, John! That's where a note would be!* However, Will was the one to quickly examine what was on the desk where it appeared that he found nothing there addressed to him.

The pair checked several of the other places one might expect to find a note, but none was overtly apparent. They then moved over to the bookcase. A book lay open on the reading stand, but again no note. They made a quick check of the rest of the house. The kitchen held a large collection of pots and pans, metal utensils, ceramic cups and containers, a few glasses tucked back in a safe place, pewter mugs, and assortments of tins, plates and cookware. The larder seemed as big as John's kitchen and was filled with higher quality items.

Upstairs in the bedrooms Ron saw stuffed mattresses, down comforters, pillows, and fine shoes and clothing. Pipes and a jar of tobacco were on one small dresser. Seemingly not wishing to intrude, John merely glanced into each room for any obvious signs of paper, but the rooms were bare of any offerings.

Will had already retreated downstairs, and Ron found him at the bookstand, leafing through the volume it held open, as though searching for something in particular. "Mister Hart, Aunt Jane has read to me from these *Songs and Sonnets* since I was little, and now I can read it by myself. She says that I may borrow it sometime when I'm a little older. There's one poem about a spider and a bee that I like... do you want to hear it?"

"Certainly, Will, but I can't say as I'll understand it."

"Oh, it is easy. Here, I think it's... Oh, I've found it."

John peered over his shoulder for a moment, and Ron had a glimpse of the title and first lines. Again, it was illegible, but:

> How by a kiffe he found both his life and death
>   Nature that gaue the Bee fo feat a grace,

Became:

> How by a kiss he found both his life and death
>   Nature that gave the Bee so apt a grace,

As Will read aloud, the lines continued,

> "To find honey of so wondrous fashion:
>   Hath taught..."

"Same," whispered John suddenly as he was scanning the words on the page.

"What?" asked Will.

"Oh, I'm sorry Master Will, it was nothing. Please read on." But Ron could feel a certain swelling of the chest with pride as he said it.

And with a shrug, Will continued,

> "Hath taught the spider out of the same place
> To fetch poison by strange alteration
> Though this be strange, it is a stranger case,
> With one kiss by secret operation,
> Both these at once in those your lips to find,
> In change whereof, I leave my heart behind."

Will turned expectantly to John, and John stared dumbly back.

"I don't understand..." began John. *Oh, come on John, it's about...* began Ron, as Will set out to gently and patiently explain the meaning to him.

"Well, you see, he's saying that a bee makes honey out of its body, and a spider makes poison out of his body, so it's strange that they can both make two completely different things, but they're so similar otherwise. And then the man tastes both honey and poison in his lover's kiss. He thinks he's only giving a kiss, but the woman is really taking his heart."

John nodded, "You are a wiser man than I, Master Will. A wiser man, indeed."

Will suddenly looked down at his shoes and blushed. "Well, truth be told, Aunt Jane had to explain it to me, too."

"I only know the old songs, lad, and this is not one of them. But I always thought that these poems and such meant more than they said."

"They do," nodded Will, who began rifling through the pages again. "Most of these are love songs, and there are some parts that Aunt Jane said might take a while for me to really understand. But she has a favorite that I like, on page, ah, here it is. Should I read it?"

"Yes, go on," said John, but Ron could feel him shifting from foot to foot and wanting to get on to other things.

"This is titled, 'The lover complaineth that deadly sickness can not help his affection,'" and he read on,

> "The enemy of life, decayer of all kind,
> That with his cold withers away the green:
> This other night me in my bed did find:
> And offered me to rid my fever clean.
> And I did grant: so did despair me blind.
> He drew his bow, with arrows sharp and keen:
> And struck the place, where love had hit before:
> And drove the first dart deeper more and more."

John was nodding by the last line, holding his hand up against his chest. "That one, I get the meaning," he said solemnly. "That one, I get the meaning."

"Yes, it is a favorite of Aunt Jane's, but there must be something I don't ken yet, because it does not ring true to me."

"Oh, it will someday, Master Will. I'm sorry to say that it will, someday."

"It must have something to do with the love part?"

John simply nodded.

"Oh, and there's one about spring," said Will, suddenly uncomfortable and flipping the pages to the very front of the volume. That was when they discovered the note that Will's Aunt Jane had said that she would leave for him.

"The wind must have blew the other pages over it," said John.

The folded paper bore an elegant script which said: "For William. I hope I will see you in Kenilworth. Here is my attempt at a seasonal verse, and we can discuss it when next we meet. Your loving Aunt, Jane."

Will unfolded the page and read aloud—

<u>Seasons</u>

Ice leapt across the pond and tamed the brook.
Winter is content to shroud in its snow,
All acts of man. E'en streams repel the hooks.
Yet neath leaden sky, something stirs below.

Seeds sprout, sprung from winter and rough climate.
Ice newly melted suckles the green wood
To a gentle condition, most well met.
All bask under a bright and bonny hood.

But too much, and we wander in the shade.
Too little, and we eschew raindrops in glens.
This splendorous witness of all life on parade
Harkens deep respect for all we depend.

I slept into Autumn and brooked no prods
To wake, perchance Summer kept me o'er long.

It must be the time period I'm in, thought Ron, remembering his class in early English literature, *because the tone of those words seems so familiar.*

"Well, now, that is quite the poem, that is," said John, but Ron noticed that he was scratching his chin as he said it. "And your aunt wrote it all by herself?"

"Yes," said Will. "She always tells me that an idle mind is worse than idle hands, and that women weren't just meant for mending and sewing."

"I know she never shies from stating her mind," John nodded. "That much I know."

"I showed her some poems I was writing last winter, and she became so excited to see them. That's when she told me she wrote poetry too, but her husband doesn't seem much interested in it. She said we should share, and now we write verses to read to each other."

"Ah, you keep up with your learning, young Master. You don't want to end up a hunched old wheelwright like me. You want to be a magistrate or some such."

"Father wants me to be a glover like him, but I don't know. The tanning stinks something bad, and I don't think father's too pleased with the craft anyway. He keeps doing everything but making gloves."

A glover? wondered Ron. *Shakespeare's father was a glover ... And this boy is named Will? Nah, that would be too much of a coincidence. I don't even know where I am or what year it is.*

"What would you like to be then, lad?"

"Really? I think a shepherd. That way I could be in the hills and lie on my back and watch the sky all day."

"I don't think it's as simple a thing as that."

Will grinned at him. "I know, but I can dream."

"That you can, Will, that you can," said John. "We better get you started off for home," as he ushered him toward the door. John gathered up the windblown oak leaves from the floor on his way out and tossed them into the road. When they'd locked up and were heading north toward the bridge Will had mentioned, John said, "I won't let you walk home alone, Master Will. We'll wait until someone we know is passing in the same direction either from Bidford or from here, and you can join them. I've heard as there are some rough folks lingering near the bushes in some spots. Old Mister Oakley was beaten and robbed just last month."

"Then I can outrun them!" exclaimed Will.

"Yes, you can, lad. Yes, you can. But it will be for me to worry all day whether you made it home safe if you try and go alone."

They walked through the town and then across the river on a stone bridge. It reached an island over a narrower channel, and then spanned the mainstream in several more arches. Three anglers had poles planted along the downstream end of the island, and Will paused to watch them for a moment.

"Any luck, Richard?" John yelled down to them.

The man at the tip of the island turned, saw them, and waved. "Not today, John," he shouted back. "The Avon don't give 'em up too easy!"

Mention of the Avon caught Ron's attention. *Hmm, maybe...* he thought. *Wouldn't that be something?*

John waved back and he and Will carried on the short distance to the intersection with the main road. The conversation turned back to Kenilworth and the Queen, passing the time as they waited for someone they knew to travel by. Several strangers walked past on foot, and two merchant's carts rolled by, but none were apparently familiar to John. Then a cobbler pushing a cart approached from the direction that Ron took to be of Bidford, since the pair had only been interested in those heading in the same direction as the cobbler. Ron recognized the man's trade immediately because he had several samples of shoes swinging from an overhead rack, and Ron could make out the form of an upside-down foot fastened to the cart bed. "Hello, Mister Harrod!" shouted John when the man drew up beside them. Ron noticed Will glance at John, obviously wondering why he'd yelled. Ron wondered, too. The old man had a wrinkled but animated face and broke into a gap-toothed grin when he recognized John.

"'Lo, John!" he shouted back.

"Are you going to Stratford?" yelled John.

Stratford! thought Ron. *Then this could be William Shakespeare!*

The man shook his head and then cupped his hand behind an ear.

"Stratford?" shouted John again.

"Yea," shouted Mister Harrod back in reply. He then grinned and mimed walking and pointed in the direction of Stratford upriver.

"Can you…" began John, but then stopped. He grabbed Will by both shoulders, maneuvered him so that the boy stood beside Mister Harrod, and then embraced them both with one arm, pointing up the road at the same time with the other.

Mister Harrod grinned and gave an exaggerated bow to Will, and then he lightly touched the boy's shoulder, again miming a march towards Stratford.

"Thank you!" yelled John as Mister Harrod nodded and took up the handles to his cart, immediately beginning to walk away up the road.

"Mister Harrod is old, but he will be a safe companion for you, Master Will," said John.

"Thank you, Mister Hart," said Will. "I hope to see you soon. Perhaps in Kenilworth?"

"Or after, lad. Or after. You stay close to Mister Harrod, now, you hear?"

"I shall," said Will, now running a bit to catch up with the gentleman who was much sprier than he had first appeared. Ron could hear the constant patter of the boy as the pair moved away, his words falling on the deafest of ears.

As John recrossed the bridge and headed toward his shop, Ron's mind was awhirl. *The boy likes poetry, lives in Stratford-upon-Avon, and his father is a glover. Still, the timing could be off by a century or two for all I know. Now, who were Shakespeare's relatives? His father was John and his mother, Mary... Did he have an Aunt Jane? If only I knew more British history, or remembered more about Shakespeare's life. I have his biography sitting on my bookshelf at home, but I only skimmed it for a paper on his wife, Anne Hathaway.* Ron was suddenly overwhelmed with frustration. *Or if I had a fucking computer and Google right now!*

John walked on, oblivious to the one-sided conversation going on somewhere inside him—Ron's patter also bouncing off deaf ears.

John's pace suddenly sped up as they approached his shop, and then he broke into a run. Both he and Ron had noticed more smoke than expected leaking through the upper cracks in the structure. John yanked the door open, and Ron could see that the upper half of the shop was now filled with smoke. A pile of wood and shavings several feet away from the firepit were the source, and the eddies of wind that followed them in caused the smoldering pile to finally burst into flame.

John wasted no time. He dashed for a bucket and then ran to a barrel that sat just outside the shop door, plunging the container down into the water and quickly hauling it to where he could empty it onto the eager flames. Ron felt totally frustrated and wished that he could help or stand outside and sound the alarm. Luckily there was no need for extra hands, and John had the fire out after several more bucketsful.

Satisfied that there was no more chance of the fire re-kindling, John began to examine the floor around the wet wood chips, and found interest in several footprints that did not match his own. The intermittent tracks seemed to lead out of the shop and onto the road, but became lost in the confusion of those made by others in passing.

Returning to the shop, John took a flat wooden shovel, and carried mounds of the offending, blackened chips out to spread along the road until there was nothing but bare ground where the pile had been made. When he finished, John stood in the doorway slowly swinging his head back and forth as he was obviously pondering who could have staged the blaze. He was shaking his head as he set back to work.

Ron was surprised at the pragmatic attitude John had taken toward the emergency. There had been no sense of panic during the fire, more of a calculated effort, and Ron could sense only mild frustration in him when the cleanup was completed. John's eyes hadn't darted about looking for a suspect, his fists had never clenched, and his breathing seemed to be normal after the fire. *Amazing,* thought Ron. *John took care of that business and accepts that there are no real clues that will lead to the culprits, otherwise he'd be out on the streets. I'm still surprised that he didn't let his emotions get the better of him, though. Which is something that would surely have happened to me. Still, I'm betting he has his suspicions about who set the blaze...*

Chapter 18.

The atmosphere in the tavern felt immediately different to Ron. John must have sensed it too, because after greeting a few friends near the door, he kept his focus straight ahead and walked purposefully up to the short wooden counter.

"Evening, John," said the tavern keeper. "A draught for you?" he asked, but then continued in a whisper, "you noticed the Webb brothers are here?"

John nodded and then said, "One of your finest, as usual, William."

Ron had no idea who the Webb brothers could be, or what their presence in the tavern meant, but he stayed alert. John didn't seem as concerned. He waited patiently for the mug to be filled, took a taste, complimented William on the quality of this keg, and then sauntered over to his usual spot near the fire. He turned his chair to face into the hearth, crossed his legs near the grate, his hands across his belly, and stared into the flames.

It didn't take long for Ron to discover who the Webb brothers were.

"Lazing about as usual, are we John?" asked an annoying voice directly behind him.

"Just enjoying a fire, Thomas," replied John. "As I think you have."

Ron tried to turn around to get a look at Thomas, but was, of course, unable to do so. *Then he thinks this guy was the one who started the fire in his shop,* he thought.

"I don't know what you mean, John. Me and Clive have been over there enjoying our ale. Till you walks in, that is."

There was a pause, and then a tap on John's shoulder. Rather than tension, Ron could sense a relaxing of John's muscles, and then the wheelwright gave a sigh. "If it wasn't to enjoy a fire, what brings you into town then, Thomas?" asked John without turning around.

"Well, our business, of course, John," came the mincing reply. "Which would have been much better if it wasn't for the meddling of that sorry cow of yours."

"God rest her soul," said John.

"Oh, she's resting all right," said Thomas, grabbing John's shoulder and trying to get him to turn around. "And well she should."

John was stouter than Ron had expected, and the heavy tug had no effect.

"God rest her soul," said John again.

"You know, if she hadn't told the tax man about our flocks, we wouldn't be in the state we're in," Thomas spat, and then pointedly, "John."

John grabbed the chair beneath him and flopped it around so that he was facing Thomas Webb. His head pulled suddenly back after he did so. "Been sampling William's fine ales now, have you, Thomas?"

"I've been drowning my sorrows, John. Same as happened to your cow, Mary."

Even Ron could feel the adrenaline course through John's system. John remained seated and outwardly relaxed, but to Ron there was the feel of a coiled spring in him.

"God rest her soul," repeated John.

Thomas kicked John's boot. "Get up, you lazy bugger. I have something to give you."

"All right, gentlemen," said William from his new position after he'd walked up behind Thomas. Ron could make out that he was carrying a short club in his right hand.

"We'll have none of that in here. If you want to do your talking, do it outside."

"Let's do just that then," said Thomas as a challenge.

John stood, but took no steps and said nothing.

"Let's go," growled Thomas.

"Mister Webb, I believe you've had too much, and won't take too much. I say we just get about our own business," John said softly.

"Because of your wife, my business is your business," said Thomas.

John nodded. "And where has your brother got to?" he asked.

"Oh, I expect he's about. Let's go."

William stepped aside as Thomas headed for the door, and Ron was sure that William gave John a wink as he passed by him, following Thomas out of the tavern.

The light had faded, but Ron, and thus John, could still see clearly enough. A man stood unsteadily to the side of the door and was rolling up his sleeves. Ron guessed that this was Thomas's brother. Thomas was doing the same.

"You know, Thomas, I'll say it again. Mary never told the taxman nothing about you. She merely said that the Smiths were being taxed for sheep they never owned. The count went with them having a bigger herd than they expected, and you, their neighbors, having a much smaller herd."

"Same as grassing us out," said the brother from several feet away.

"Same as setting him on us," said Thomas.

"I think you're letting your ale do your thinking for you," said John. "The only reason I'm standing here is to help you remember not to play with fire." He relaxed again and let his big hands rest down by his thighs. To Ron's surprise, John must have anticipated the coming blow, but did little in defense. Ron felt like he was trying to back out of John's skull as the fist came towards him, and John did feint back a tad as he took a light jolt to the chin.

"Clive, you need to keep your distance," said John without turning from Thomas, who landed another harder punch to John's tight stomach.

"Thomas," began John when Clive suddenly jumped from beside John to try and wrap up the stout man's arms. John pushed out with an open hand into Clive's chest and sent the man flying backward.

"As I was saying, Thomas, you need to settle down and take your brother home."

Thomas had his arm back for another attempt when John stretched out with a fist that caught the flesh of Thomas's ear. The same hand that was aiming for John suddenly clasped that side of his head. John immediately followed with his opposite fist and caught the opposite ear. Thomas took a step back, dropped both hands into fists and lunged at John. Ron was preparing for the worst, although he could only feel a dulled version of the pain John must have been experiencing from the physical attacks. John seemed to know what he was doing though. He brought up his fist during his opponent's midstride and caught the first ear with an upward motion, this time separating some of the lobed end of the ear from the head.

Ron was confused. It seemed to him that one solid blow from John could separate Thomas's head from his body, but he was using each jab as an increasingly noticeable warning. Ron was sure that if it was him with the physical advantage, he would probably be trying to beat some revenge for the fire into Thomas. He found himself impressed with the amount of restraint that John was showing.

The hit hadn't stopped Thomas's forward momentum and a fist came up under John's chin just before the shepherd slammed into John's chest. John took him by both shoulders and shoved him back. Thomas staggered but didn't fall, and Clive was on his feet by this time, too, joining his brother. The two scrappers were poised for an all-out onslaught when they were flooded with light from the tavern door. Several shadows swept out across the road, and John was suddenly flanked by five patrons.

"It's time to go home, lads," John said to the pair.

"Good thing we was here to rescue poor Mister Hart," said a voice next to him.

Six men erupted in laughter while two made some rude gestures and stomped off into the night, one holding a hand to the side of his head.

"How many times is that now?" asked the man who had told the joke.

"Three at least, James. Three at least," as those remaining turned and filed back into the tavern.

"Ain't it funny," said James, clapping John on the back. "The falser the charge, the harder it sticks."

It was dark when John's eyes shut, doubling the reason Ron could see nothing, but he could hear the man's heavy breathing and vaguely feel the hard bed beneath him. He thought about the altercation, and how, except for that first blow, it felt the entire time that he himself was watching it from afar. It still felt strange to be in a body with filtered sensations and absolutely no control over its actions.

And then he remembered. *I may have met William Shakespeare today! The Western world's premier poet... just a boy starting off on such a gifted path. I need to spend more time with him!* He considered some of the ramifications of this encounter, and hoped that it wasn't merely by chance that they'd met. *Well, maybe 'met' is a little bit of a stretch,* he admitted to himself.

At this thought, his frustration at being unable to interact with Will himself began to take over. *What's the point of being here if I can't even talk to him?* he wondered. The possibilities of the things he could learn from William Shakespeare brought to mind the obvious comparisons between what he had written in his life and The Bard's impressive corpus. This then led to thoughts of his own 'career' next to that of the great playwright and it didn't look good at all. Ron's mood turned sour.

My path has been a descent into a Dantesque Bad Poet's Circle of Hell. I get a Mediocre Muse whispering in my ear, the reactions to my blog are all milquetoast and totally unhelpful, my printed collections garnered zero sales. Now, here I am consigned to being powerless inside some illiterate lout, and getting to meet but have no contact with a true genius—a leaky dingy rocking in the wake of the Queen Mary.

With the image of being in a small boat alone on a vast ocean in mind, he thought, *No one hears me. Not at home through my poems. Not here where I'm invisible and can't say a word out loud. And no one has heard of me. I'll die an unknown—sailing alone off the edge of this strangely flat world.*

He lay there for a few moments and then was suddenly overcome by an agonizing bout of claustrophobia. Almost like a drowning man who is sinking and then suddenly realizes that he will never again reach the surface. He screamed out into emptiness, tried to turn around, open the man's eyes, move his arms—anything to show that he was alive, that he had some control of his surroundings. *Let me out!* He screamed again and again. Nothing in nothingness - except now for a gentle snoring.

Ron's main worry was that he would go mad, and in fact, he was convinced that he briefly had that night.

Chapter 19.

RON, ALONG with John, awoke to the crow of little Alice's rooster a few houses away and strong morning light pouring into the house through all the various chinks and cracks. Ron, feeling incredibly hollow, but in a much better mood, nearly laughed to himself as he attempted a yawn with no physical means of doing so. John threw off the coarse linen cover, sat up rubbing his face, and rose to rummage in one of his two chests at the end of the bed. Opening the chest on the right he took out a clean linen shirt and set it on the bed. He closed this, and then turned and opened the chest on the left. On the top was a quilt, and below lay several woolen blankets and a few more linen bed covers. John reached down and lifted this pile and set it on top of the right-hand chest.

Ron found himself peering to see what was inside, but John's eyes knew what to expect. At the bottom of the chest were folded a woman's shawl along with a rust-colored bodice, a blouse and blue skirt. A small wooden cross attached to a leather thong was arranged on top of these. To Ron's surprise, John reached in, set the cross aside, roughly took hold of the entire bundle of clothing, and drew it up to his face where he paused, and then breathed in deeply. He held it there for several minutes, gently breathing in and out, and then slowly replaced all the contents of the chest in the proper order. Closing the lid, Ron heard John mutter, "God rest her soul."

The clothing and John's deeply heartfelt attachment made it easy for Ron to work out that Mary must have been John's wife and that she had somehow drowned, based on Thomas Webb's comment from the previous evening. He wondered how long ago this had happened and began to appreciate the shallows leading to the depth of John's grief.

None of this morning's actions were part of the routine Ron had witnessed over the past several days, and he wondered what was up. They had arisen later than normal, and now John seemed more hurried. He took the shirt off the bed and descended the stairs, Ron trying, half-heartedly now, to somehow induce a slip or a fall. At the bottom, John turned to the kitchen where he filled a basin from a pail and washed his face and hands in the water, taking care around the still tender wound on his forehead. He took up a wooden comb and stroked and scratched it through his hair until he was satisfied. Returning to the living area, he stripped off his nightshirt and donned the clean shirt, next walking over to the end of the house and retrieving a pair of clean woolen trousers off a short stand which stood next to the fire pit.

What's going on? wondered Ron when, simultaneously, he made out the peal of the church bells in the distance. *Ah, this is Sunday, and John is going to church,* realized Ron as John pulled on his pants, rubbed his hands through his hair again, and then headed back toward the kitchen. Cutting a section of bread, chewing bites hurriedly, and downing glugs of the weak beer in between, John was soon standing at the door and examining himself as best he could without a mirror. *He must be obsessed with his hair,* thought Ron as John again scratched his scalp and ruffled his hair. *Or maybe lice,* he thought on reflection, giving what in his physical body might have been a shudder. John patted about his clothing and gave a final brushing off of his chest to ensure that there were no lingering crumbs. Satisfied, he then opened his front door and stepped out into the morning sunshine.

He was at the end of the lane and trailing the line of villagers heading toward the Sunday service. Half-way to the church he caught up with Alice and her mother who was hiking her skirts up to avoid as much of the mud as possible. "Good morning, Mistress Allen," said John as he strode up and grabbed Alice's hand evoking a big smile from the girl.

"Ah, a fine morning it is, Mister Hart, isn't it?" asked Alice's mother looking about at the sun-washed landscape.

"That it is, Mistress. Allen, that it is," said John. "How are the pair of you fine ladies getting on?"

"Very well, Mister Hart. The hens are laying, and I can't keep up with the sewing, so this looks to be a fine spring and summer."

"That is so good to hear," said John. "Lucky you to have Miss Alice to help you with the hens."

Both Alice and Mrs. Allen grinned broadly at this, and Mrs. Allen nodded, giving him a wink of appreciation. The small talk that followed centered mainly on the egg production of the layers.

They had turned off the main road at The Bell tavern, which Ron now recognized, and after a short stretch between some low houses, were soon climbing the few steps up to the churchyard where they followed the line of Sunday worshippers entering the parish church dominated by a square stone belltower. Gravestones were situated on both sides of the walkway, and John bowed his head toward a spot among those to the left.

Mary's grave, thought Ron as he found himself thinking that he would need to visit this town when he returned to his own place and time, the unlikelihood of which caused a momentary bout of anxiety.

Upon entering the huge hall, Mrs. Allen and Alice had caught up with some friends and joined the ladies to the left of the central aisle, and John chose a seat near the rear on the right. The tavern keeper, William, joined him as the ceremonies began and the doors were pulled shut. He greeted John with a nod, and the pair sat comfortably side-by-side indicating to Ron that this was their accustomed spot.

John, and thus Ron, surveyed the congregation from the back. Prominent families and the more well-to-do populated the foremost pews, and then the single and simpler men and ladies filled out the remainder of the benches. His eyes lit on a familiar profile. Toward the rear of the women's seating, Ron recognized Mrs. Jones. John's eyes seemed to linger there, when she suddenly turned and gave him a quick smile.

After the first song, William nudged John in the side. In a low voice he whispered, "You should go over and sit with the widow Jones, John. I think she's caught your eye." John gave a little smile, but shook his head in reply. *Ah, so she's a widow,* thought Ron, now making more sense of the encounter between John and Mrs. Jones in his workshop.

Being one of the last in, John was also one of the last outside after the service. Keeping his head bowed, he'd waited his turn as those in the forward rows made their way down the aisle ahead of him. Once through the huge door, he turned away from the main walk, strolling across the grass to the side of the church instead of heading directly for home. From his demeanor, Ron could tell that this was a customary practice for the man on Sundays. John walked to a far row of gravestones and stopped before one that read: *Here lies Mary Hart beloved wife, 1536—1571.* He lowered his head for a few moments, leaned down to pluck a few of spring's new weeds from the thick grass, patted the stone affectionately, and then turned back toward the remaining congregants who were mingling and socializing before the cathedral.

That confirms that he's a widower, thought Ron, *and has probably been one for at least a few years. So, Mary was... thirty-five when she died, and John seems to be in his mid-forties. The present time is at least a few years after 1571. What is that? The reign of Elizabeth?* Ron again cursed himself for not knowing more of British history.

John had taken several steps in the direction of the central walkway when he suddenly pivoted and headed toward a lone figure standing before a gravestone situated nearer the rear of the church. Ron soon saw that this was Mrs. Jones who was now kneeling and crossing herself. As John approached, Ron could see that the burial sites in this section were much newer than the area Mary had been buried in, and little vegetation had grown on the mound Mrs. Jones now knelt beside.

"Good morning, Missus Jones," said John with a certain tenderness. "Did you enjoy today's sermon?"

Mrs. Jones turned to look up at him with a sad smile. "Yes. It seems that we all must work even harder to avoid sinning in God's eyes, mustn't we?"

"That we must," said John without the usual repetition that Ron was now accustomed to hearing.

John suddenly reached out and gave Mrs. Jones' shoulder a squeeze, and she in turn held a hand against John's calf. Then, in what must have been a measure of decorum, John stepped back a pace. Mrs. Jones pivoted to face the grave and suddenly burst into tears. John stood by her side until they passed. She wiped her eyes on her smock and then gave him another, more melancholy look.

"I am so sorry that your poor Richard passed so suddenly," John said in a low voice. "But there are ways to make us both happier."

Mrs. Jones suddenly gave him a look of reproach and hissed, "Mister Hart. This is hardly the time nor the place!"

Now he's done it, thought Ron.

John's hands immediately flew out with palms extended. "No, no, that's not what I meant at all, you silly cow," he said softly. "I meant what we discussed this winter. That you and I could put both of our griefs behind us by making things respectable under God." He stepped in closer. "Mary liked Richard, and Richard, Mary, and so I don't think either of them would mind our being together."

Mrs. Jones turned back to the headstone that Ron could see put the death of Mr. Jones at October of 1573, two years after Mary had passed away. "I just need a little more time, John. Some of the other women are already starting to make comments about me not showing the proper grieving," as she glanced over at the retreating crowd.

"As you wish, ma'am, as you wish," said John as he gave her shoulder another squeeze and then headed for home.

To Ron, their conversations and demeanors witnessed during the tryst in the shop and this meeting in the graveyard seemed to be completely at odds, but then he realized that he knew nothing about the customs during this age. He guessed that there could be a huge difference between public and private personas. Or it could simply be the familiar matter of two individuals dealing with both grief and love at the same time.

Chapter 20.

JOHN ATE and rested over the midday hours. Ron, in the meantime, reflected on last night's panic attack. In a moment of clarity, he saw that the episode was due, in large part, to his feeling of total anonymity. He was, of course, completely isolated here within John's world, but he also knew that the seeds of panic had been sown in Madison. Despite his introverted nature, he craved attention and approval and he saw that if he were more self-assured about his writing, the attack might not have been nearly as severe, or have even occurred in the first place.

He then devoted his time to wondering, *Why am I here?* The aftermath of being the previous night's straight-jacketed inmate had left him resigned to his lot being stuck with John, but he was still curious as to his purpose here. He had, of course, questioned the meaning of his existence when he was a teenager, but that was in the broader context of why <u>we</u> were here—why humans existed in the first place. This time his question was much more specific. *Is this what happens when you die? We're each thrown into another person's experience to learn from them? Then what is the point of all of this? If I was sent here to learn something, what the hell is it? I can hardly see that being trapped in the life of some poor wheelwright is of any use. Why wasn't I dropped into someone of consequence? A duke or a knight or someone like that? Why not Shakespeare for Christ's sake? What am I learning from John? I'm melded to him, in absolute lockstep. Everything he does affects and captivates me, but I have absolutely no impact on him whatsoever. Where's the logic to all of this?*

He spent some time thinking carefully about everything he'd experienced thus far in case a lesson had been provided and he'd missed it. *Maybe it was to do with Shakespeare after all, if that's who Will was. As I wondered before, maybe I was sent here to meet or learn something from the great William Shakespeare. If so, then why aren't I spending more time with him? And he's just a boy learning about poetry himself—how could he pass on anything at this age? And where is he?*

Since he expected that he might be in historic England for some time to come, he resolved to keep his eyes open for any possible teachable moments that might fulfill his purpose here and let him get the hell out.

The afternoon's events caught Ron totally by surprise. He'd expected John to return to the workshop when he again stepped outside, but instead of opening the shop door, John passed it by. He was heading to either the tavern or back to church, or at least Ron guessed as much, since he was following the same route they'd taken that morning. Rather than the pealing of the church bells as accompaniment, however, Ron began to make out the strains of a fiddle as they climbed the few steps up to the churchyard. *Music! Live music!* Ron shouted, and the tune became louder as John rounded the church to the large open field of grass that lay behind. The entire town appeared to have turned out at the green and was gathered in what Ron thought must have been... *a fete,* he finally decided, trying to put an older term to the block party they came upon.

Tables and benches were spread along one side, and activity abounded: children ran about trailing ribbons; some were over among the back section of the churchyard, which was peppered with gravestones, playing the familiar game of hide-and-go-seek; some of the older children were throwing hoops at a stake to see who could ring it; and a group of men were rolling heavy balls across the grass toward a smaller ball. *What's the name of that game? Starts with a 'b,'* wondered Ron, coming up empty. All around were small groups as at any party, drinking and laughing. John was headed for a stout table which boasted two large round kegs manned by William from the tavern. A spare keg sat on the grass behind him.

"William," said John, nodding his head as he slapped his hands on the table.

"John," greeted William, as he twisted the tap, filling a pewter mug which he then set before his friend.

"Ah, God, this is good," said John as he took a healthy drink of the frothy beer.

"Befitting the wonderful day, wouldn't you say?" asked William.

"That it does, William. That it does," said John looking about. Ron gave an inner sigh at John's predictable speech pattern. "It's been a long winter, hasn't it? And this being the perfect weather for the wake."

"And in welcoming the Queen herself to Kenilworth up north just next week. A new Hocktide! Are you going, John?"

John shook his head. "No, and neither are many from around these parts, I would wager. Who could afford it and where would a body stay?"

William gave a broad smile. "That's why we're here!" he exclaimed, raising his own tankard, and smashing it into John's so that ale rose and slopped out of both mugs.

John took another huge drink from his tankard, but happened to glance up while doing so. His attempted swallowing of the mouthful of ale, while simultaneously saying, "Oh!" proved to be too difficult for his throat and resulted in much coughing while William came around the table and slapped his back. Ron wondered what had John so flustered as the man recovered and set his mug down on the table. "Just a moment, William," he said as he wiped foam off his mouth, and dabbed at his tearing eyes. He self-consciously patted down his clothing, ran his hands through his hair, and then walked slowly, but purposefully, over to a well-dressed couple who were just finishing a conversation with the vicar. Ron recognized Mistress Jane from the reading lesson. "Mister Barnwell, and Mistress," John said while giving a bow to his head. "How was your trip to Henley?"

"Ah, John," said Mister Barnwell, tilting his head in welcome and reaching over to pat John's shoulder. "Yes, it was fine, just fine. I have found a new buyer for this year's wool, and a supplier of some more lambs for this summer. It went very well indeed."

"That is good news," said John as he drew the set of skeleton keys from his pocket and reached out to hand it to Mister Barnwell.

"No, John, you keep this set if you don't mind. We leave for Kenilworth tomorrow, and I'd like you to look after the house again while we're gone."

John nodded, and then turning to Mistress Barnwell said, "I hope it is all right, as I let young Master Shakespeare into the house to look for a poem he was expecting?"

Ah ha! So, it definitely is William Shakespeare! thought Ron, finally getting confirmation . *Let's go see him, John. Stratford-upon-Avon can't be that far away, can it?*

"Oh, yes!" she exclaimed excitedly. "Did he read it? Did he like it?"

"Yes, Mistress, I would say he did. Very much so."

"Oh, good!" she said. "Did he leave me anything?"

"No, Mistress."

Her eyes showed disappointment, but she kept her smile. "He really does have a natural talent, do you know? We just need to nurture it and let it grow."

"I'm sure he does," said John, "I'm sure he does."

Of course he does! shouted Ron. *John, this boy will come to be the epitome of what a poet is!* To no avail.

"Enjoy the wake, now," said John as a couple came up to speak with the Barnwells. Bowing as he went, John retreated back to his mug of ale.

❧

The musicians had finished a slow introductory number, and now launched into a lively tune with pipes, drums, and fiddle. Many of those nearby started clapping along in time with the beat, and a young couple jumped up to dance, or so Ron thought. The pair faced each other, stamping feet and clapping, but that was all for the moment. Soon others were up and joining them until a line of six women faced a similar one of men. At some cue, the dance began. Several similar groups flowered around them until most of those in the immediate area were up and joining in.

John had moved to the side of the table since a rush toward the ale had occurred before the dancing began in earnest. He was tapping his foot to the music, and Ron could tell that although he might be game, John had a poor sense of rhythm so he was certain that John would never participate.

"So, are you joining in?" William asked John.

John replied with a broad grin.

"Oh ho!" laughed William.

Wow, not what I expected at all, thought Ron.

John made no immediate moves to find a partner, and the two men surveyed the dancers.

"So, who do you think is the best out there, John? The Buckleys certainly are a dashing couple, and the Barnwells are also very elegant."

"George and Claire," said John without hesitation.

"Where are they?" asked William as he searched the dancers. "Oh, there," apparently finding them in a group to the left. "Why, they barely stand out at all."

"I know," said John. "They're the best."

"Now why do you say that?"

"Well, watch them for a moment and then the rest. The Buckleys and the Barnwells are dancing to be seen. They're always watching others watching them, barely paying attention to their partners. The Martins over there are just the opposite. They're too worried about what others think to dance at all. Now look at young George and Claire. They're listening to the music, they're paying attention to each other, to their place in the line, and to how they move. But more than that, they're happy at this moment, as if there is nothing else in the world. They are the dance. More than any of the others."

William observed them for a spell and then apparently found that he had to nod in agreement. "Well, right you are, John."

Ron found himself taken aback at John's insight. The man said little, and even Ron couldn't read his thoughts to know his mind, so Ron had, admittedly, taken the man as somewhat dim. He had no idea which couple was George and Claire—suspecting that they were the first pair that had rushed up for the dance—but trusted John's perceptive take on the couple. *Hmm, quiet and observant is our John. Maybe I've misjudged him.*

Then John caught sight of Mrs. Jones, who was standing to the side with two friends some distance away. They each exchanged glances several times, appeared unsure, but then both dipped their heads in agreement. John set down his tankard and the pair drifted together and then over to squeeze into the middle of a line, positioning themselves opposite from one another. *Ah,* thought Ron, *a socially acceptable way to spend some time together.*

Ron was not much of a dancer himself, especially in these structured folk dances, and he could see that it would take several sessions before he could have followed the pattern well enough to join in—if forced to do so. John, on the other hand, seemed to know the moves and was much better at it than Ron would have guessed. The dance involved the pairs at each end alternately meeting in the middle and then returning to their respective places several times, and then all of the pairs joining hands, moving along the line, parting, and rejoining in different combinations until a new couple was at the end of the line where it started all over again. Somehow, John seemed to be sparked each time he took the hand of Mrs. Jones, and Ron sensed that the same thing was happening to his partner.

Many of the faces in the crowd were becoming familiar to Ron, and he was amazed to see the Webb brothers enjoying themselves and even dancing next to John on occasion. There was no hint of the animosity witnessed at the tavern, and Ron could detect no unease on John's part. John partnered with Mrs. Allen during one of the circle dances and, in another, Alice teetered delightedly on his shoulders as they whirled around.

Ron found that his mind was blank and he was completely wrapped up in the festive atmosphere and camaraderie that surrounded him. *Maybe the reason I'm here is that this is where I should be—somehow falling into the right people, time, and place—no grander purpose after all,* thought Ron with a feeling of contentment he hadn't had for some time and, oddly, of being a part of the village, among friends—without them even being aware that he was there.

Excitement erupted during the next music number. The Barnwells were in the middle of a line dance when Mistress Jane suddenly swooned and was luckily caught by the woman Ron guessed was Claire just as she fell. The music stopped, and a small crowd gathered to watch or give aid. Mistress Jane was soon back on her feet—looking incredibly pale, but waving off help and reassuring the crowd that there was no need to fuss. Despite her rosy self-assessment, however, Ron soon noticed Mister Barnwell, Martha, and another woman helping Mistress Jane walk slowly across the green toward home.

Ron was left flabbergasted by the stamina of these people. Sure, there were individual breaks for food and drink, but John and Mrs. Jones were no different from the others in sticking with it for hours until the red sun was finally winking at them from the western horizon. They had danced in lines, in circles, and there had been rowdy stomping by some of the drunker among them near the end. All three of William's kegs were standing on the table, spigot up. William himself had joined in the dancing for the last half hour with a woman Ron had seen helping out at the tavern. The band was flagging at the end, but gave a rousing final tune. Ron could see steam rising off of many of the dancers as the air around them quickly cooled without the sun to warm it. The youngest children who were already curled up on some felt rugs under blankets were being gathered up by their mothers. The fading light was followed by a stream of fellowship heading back around the church and toward home. Ron caught no sign of Mrs. Jones after the two had parted with a smile, but Ron could still notice a spring in John's step as he hummed the main song that had played on and off throughout the afternoon, albeit off-key.

As John went through his evening chores and made ready for bed, Ron reflected on the day. He was an extreme introvert by nature and hated large social gatherings, but had thoroughly enjoyed John's participation in the fete. Somehow, being confined to John's body for so long with no contact with any personal friends, or even fellow residents of Madison, for that matter, had left Ron pining for a gathering of any sort in which he could take part. Socializing was so easy for John, and now Ron saw that simply joining in was more than half the battle—and that it shouldn't even be a battle at all—it should be, and was, enjoyable. It was community.

For the first time since his arrival, Ron fell into a deep sleep at the same moment John's head hit the pillow. He had a single dream that he would recall the next morning.

In it, he had been back home in Madison and perusing his bookshelf until he found a signed copy of 'Steel Trees' by his friend Nathan Goldblatt that, evident from a badge on the front, had won a national book award. His friend had always written edgier, more politically relevant, and topical poetry than Ron, and he saw its general appeal. He flipped through the book and chose a poem at random.

Egotripping

We dwell in the gut of something ravenous
That sups at a never-ending table of sumptuous
    delights,
Yet we pay no mind to what lands before us.
We choose instead to dine upon each other,
Feasting on more intimate, nervier things.
Yeast in a bowl, we won't stop till we're dead

Grabbing up iron for protection
But torn apart by lead.
The best of us attempt to see beyond
Trying to focus on the dim rumor of a distant light
While the rest squint through greasy goggles
For a glimpse of smeared smiles in the mirror.
Pleased with what we see.
Those few who leave us behind
Scrabble up a flint sharp hill
Sacrificing shoes and toes, gloves and fingers, pants
    and knees
Till reaching the top they are barely there,
If there at all.
We are as equally curious as they.
We ask,
What does that have to do with us?

Chapter 21.

WHAT AN odd thing to dream, thought Ron in darkness, unsure of the time. *And odder still to have a dream while dreaming—if that's what this experience here has been...*

John awoke moments later at first light and was still humming a mangled rendition of the same tune from the previous evening as he dressed for the day and headed downstairs, this time much more cavalierly than since Ron's spectacular arrival. Ron made no attempt to topple him, being now familiar with the futility of his actions. John had secreted some pasties in his pockets before he'd departed the fete, and ate them for breakfast, not bothering to cook a meal this morning.

Once in the shop, he stoked a larger fire than normal to warm the space up, and immediately set to work. The spokes were all arranged around the hub, and now came the task of attaching the outer rim. There were, by Ron's count, six outer rim sections to be attached to the spokes. As with the hub, the mortises needed to be finalized to receive each of the spokes, and John would chisel out each for a good match and then hammer the pre-formed semi-circle onto the awaiting spokes. Each curved segment was positioned so that a portion overlapped with the previous one. When two had been attached, they were married to each other with a series of pegs at the overlap, and so on until the wheel was completed.

Although fully absorbed in the process and experience at the beginning, Ron became bored by the repetition, and for the one of the few times since landing in England, was able to completely break away from the daytime activities around him and retreat into his own thoughts. *It's like I've become immersed in a 4K, surround sound, 3-D screening of the most engaging, intimate program ever made. I just can't look away. But what is this, really?* He suddenly felt it peculiar that at this point in a normal musing, he might have sat down on a chair, gone out for a contemplative stroll, or walked over to a window to stare out into the distance, but instead John just kept working away at his wheel. *Hmm,* observed Ron. *John's absorption in his task is really no different than me getting lost in soldering circuits back at Crone Amplifiers. Here I thought all this time that his work was mindless, but after hearing him at the fete yesterday, I'd love to know what he's thinking about right now. I'm sure it's not just about this repetitive work or Mrs. Jones.*

And then he reflected on his past in the Madison that, strangely, was in these people's future. He found himself lamenting that he hadn't taken his relationship with Sara more seriously. Once Sara had returned to Madison from both Nathan and Chicago, they'd been immediately physically attracted to one another and had gradually become best friends. But he'd taken her for granted, like a mere roommate, and Ron wondered whether the dream he'd just had about egotism was germane, bringing to the surface the fact that much of his focus had always been on himself. He knew that he would never find a better match on the planet than Sara. As he thought about it, he realized that the concept of a match with her wasn't even meaningful. She'd changed his life—its entire trajectory since he'd met her had been in a unique and positive direction, which was markedly different than the out of control, flaming-plane-falling-out-of-the-sky disaster that it had been before they'd become a couple. She had literally made him what he was—not as some strived-for success, but as a whole person. And now she was no longer in his reality. Ron, as if he could breathe, suddenly felt like the air was sucked out of him—as if he'd stepped into a vacuum chamber just as the heavy metal doors slammed shut. Still no panic, however. More of the icy feeling of deep regret one might get for the briefest moment when ejected helmetless in empty space.

To take his mind off this thread, he went to his poetry. Here he was, living within John's reality during the time of William Shakespeare, of all people, and he perceived the almost mystical importance that poetry, of the written word, held for Will and Mistress Jane. It was like a secret language between them—something neither of them seemed to share with anyone else. John could hardly read or spell, there was no paper or pen to be had anywhere, except in Mistress Jane's home. And in that house, there was only one, single, solitary book of poetry. He'd tried to scan the few volumes on the bookshelf, whenever John looked in that direction, and he'd noticed a few bibles, some family histories, several of what appeared to be treatises on medicine, religion, or, to him, extremely arcane subjects. But, *Songs and Sonnets* was the only book of poetry among them, and that printing was possibly the only collection of poems available in the entire kingdom, for all Ron knew.

He thought back to his blog, and he was suddenly filled with his old anger. He felt like storming the castle of the publishing world. *We have all of those things. We have shelves of resources, reams of paper, piles of pens, and computers and printers in every house. Why are there gatekeepers—the literary agents and arbitrary obstacles to entrance? Why can't we flood the world with poems? Can there be too many?* Ron soon worked himself into composing another diatribe to post on his website—if he ever saw it again, that was. But, somehow, this frustration and his mental rant faded into the background as he watched

John finish his task. This surprised him somewhat, and he wondered whether the ability to publicly air his grievances somehow fanned the flames of his indignation. That his bluster was there only if he had a soapbox? That he subconsciously created his own feedback loop for the attention? *Nah*, he thought. *I'm not that egocentric.*

It suddenly seemed a little brighter in the shop, and when John threw open the door, he stared into the last sliver of the setting sun which was finally peeking out from underneath the heavy, black clouds that had been gathering from the east all afternoon.

Chapter 22.

RON **AWOKE** to darkness and tried to open his eyes. *Oh, they are open—John's are still closed*, he thought and listened to the few remaining drops hit the floor following the torrents that had raked the roof last night, revealing several leaks through the thatching in the process. He then realized that he'd had another dream and he remembered that it had been a strange one even as he felt it slipping away from him. He tried to grasp it, but all he could recall was a woman entering a room. *I'd been in an adjacent room, but the walls had turned as transparent as glass when she entered hers. She'd walked up to the wall between us, but acted like she was looking into a mirror and couldn't see me. She took out a tube of bright red lipstick and started to apply it to her lips. I'd shouted and pounded on the wall as hard as I could, but she had no idea I was there.*

He lay in the darkness and a poem, or something like one, formed as he waited for John to wake for the day.

<u>KOOL WON</u>

Black flecks fall from the lashes
She leans in closer
Vapor blooms and fades with each breath
The brush pushes up and the lashes spring down
Now the lipstick, smeared and finished with a gentle
  purse
She steps back, admiring her work,
Then twists the tube, and writes:
TAP
On the mirror

PAT
Comes out on the other side
Her focus switches
To something behind the mirror
She frowns
YAWA KOOL
She scrawls in brilliant red
And stalks away.

John finally stirred, and Ron could make out a blurred morning light before John rubbed his eyes to clear them and rose to greet the day. Rather than humming a tune, he started this morning off by mumbling and repeating a strange poem of his own:

Oats, herring, cheese be mine
Mister Miller is a ball of twine
Alice is a bright green ribbon
Missus Allen is sticks to knit on
William is a bag of hops
Missus Jones is a ragged mop.

After the tenth repetition, Ron had it committed to memory as well, and found himself wishing John would just shut up. *He likes Mrs. Jones,* he thought. *Why on earth would he call her a ragged mop?* The reason became clear to him as the morning progressed.

John gathered some clothing and a quilt into a string bag and set it by the door. He then prepared and ate a large breakfast of thick porridge and a boiled egg, during which time he poured some of his weak beer into a leather sack and stoppered it up. He also chose some bread, cheese, and some sort of cooked or cured meat, and stuffed all of these into a separate leather bag. Checking that all was in order, and pouring water onto the remains of the fire, he grabbed the two bags and closed up the house before heading for his workspace. The road was now a swamp from last night's storm, and John stuck close to the house, tiptoeing and sliding through the mud as he made his way to the shop.

John pulled open the workshop door to its full extent, set the bags to the side, and then slopped around the side of the shop to the back, slipping twice on the sodden grass as he did so. There sat a sturdy handcart supported by two large wheels, and from the front of the cart extended a pair of long handles with a crossbar to connect them near the end. John stooped, picked up the wet handles, and then struggled to drag the cart around to the front and set it in place before the open door.

In the shop, he turned the wheel he'd just finished around on its stand to check that it was true and that all the fastenings were secure, pushing up and down as he did so to check for rattles or loose spokes. Satisfied, he grabbed two of the spokes near the hub, squatted, and then heaved up with an effort. The wheel came free of the stand and John held it as a weightlifter might in mid-lift, then duck-walked it over to the open door where he set it down to rest for a moment. Rehoisting the wheel, he slogged through the mud to the back of the cart where he pushed up with a grunt and had the wheel laying at an angle in the bed, as it was too wide to lay flat. He took a moment and some deep breaths before he retrieved the two bags from beside the door, stashed them in the bottom of the cart bed, and covered them with an oilcloth.

Back in the shop, John gathered up some chisels, a mallet, a spokeshave, and several other tools on a wooden tray and laid them in the back of the cart, covering these with an oilcloth as well. Checking over what was in the bed and what remained in the shop, he appeared satisfied as he pulled the shop door shut, reciting his poem aloud the entire time.

John stepped behind the crossbar, lifted the handles whose tips rested in the mud, and then strained forward with little movement from the cart. He pulled backwards and then lunged ahead, and Ron could hear the sucking sound as the mud finally released the wheels. John then began to pull the cart along the road, meeting some severe resistance at the muddiest sections.

I wonder where Mr. Pen... something lives? Ron asked himself as they set off, visualizing the name spelled with a backwards 'P'.

John was just passing Mrs. Allen's house when he noticed her letting the chickens out of their coop. He set the handles down and called a good morning to her. She answered with a similar wish, and then he said, "So, it is to be some knitting needles for you, and some..."

A loud "Hush!" from Mrs. Allen stopped him in mid-sentence. "That other thing is meant to be a surprise, Mister Hart!"

"Ah," said John, simultaneously touching the side of his nose. "And that it shall be, Missus Allen. Do you need anything else from Stratford? I should return late this afternoon or tomorrow."

Oh, Stratford, thought Ron . *Maybe we'll run into Will?* he hoped.

"No, unless you see some honey for a good price. I can pay you now if you like."

"There is no need, I'll keep an eye out."

"Thank you for picking those things up for us," she said as Alice emerged from the doorway, remaining on the stoop, out of the mud.

"What things?" the girl asked languidly, rubbing the sleep from her eyes.

"Mister Hart is going to Stratford and bringing me back some knitting needles, dearest."

"Oh!" Alice exclaimed. And then slowly and deliberately, "Can I go, too?"

"Not on this trip, Alice," said John. "But perhaps some other time."

Alice nodded as if this was to be expected and started over toward her mother who bade her stop. Mrs. Allen brought a small wooden tray of seed over to the girl so that she could feed the hens from her dry perch.

"Good day, then," said John, taking up the cart handles.

"And a safe journey to you, Mister Hart," said Mrs. Allen.

A shopping list, thought Ron, as John added an un-rhymed 'and some honey' to the end of the poem and resumed chanting it as he headed up the road.

John passed the tavern and the church on the left, and they were still far from the bridge when Ron could make out a large dark brown horse and a rider stopped where it spanned a channel to the small island. The rider seemed to have been conversing with someone down below and then urged the horse into a fast trot toward the town. John had managed a quarter of the remaining distance to the river when the rider halted beside him. The bottom half of the sweating horse was covered in mud, its tail a caked mass. "Excuse me, Sir," the rider said urgently while dismounting with a plop into the road. "Would you know where I can find John Hart?"

John stared at him for a moment and then said, "Why, that would be me."

"Good, Mister Hart!" said the rider, visibly relieved, and slaking his hold on the reins. "I thought it might be so, based on the description I was given. I am Paul Smith, and I have been sent by Master Barnwell to find you."

"And why is that, Sir?" asked John with some alarm in his voice.

"His Mistress Jane has taken very poorly, John. She was in good health on the trip to Kenilworth yesterday, but he and the apothecary there have been unable to rouse her since yesterday evening. She has no fever, but merely flutters her eyes when they try to wake her. I have been sent to fetch some articles of hers from the house to which you have the keys, and I am to try and plead with your priest to come to her side, since he is so well acquainted with her spirit."

"Oh, this is distressing news," said John, hurriedly, compared to his normal tempo. "Distressing indeed." Ron was in complete agreement, and said as much to... himself.

"And I have been told to enquire whether you could alert Jane's sisters, Mary and Mary Margaret, that she is so ill. If you are unable, I am to try and locate them after my business here is finished."

"That will be no problem for me in the least. In fact, I am on my way to Stratford at this very moment to deliver a wheel. I can speak with Mistress Shakespeare there, and then go on to Wilmcote to speak with Mistress Mary Margaret as well."

Mary—Will's mother! thought Ron. *Perhaps we'll have a chance to see Will again!*

John pulled the cart off the road and up against the nearest building before he set the handles down. "Let's us get to the Barnwell's house so that you can fetch what you need, and then I can point you to the vicar's lodgings."

Paul nodded, tugged the horse's reins, and followed John back to the Barnwell home.

They both removed their mud-caked boots on the stoop before entering the house, and once inside, Paul stopped and stared around in a daze. "What is it you have been asked to retrieve?" asked John helpfully.

"Let me see," said Paul, recovering and thinking hard about the mental list he held. "I am to fetch her bible, her mother's rosary, some fresh bedclothes, and two bottles of tinctures that have helped her in the past."

John nodded and Paul followed him about the house as he collected the various items. They had trouble selecting the proper vials, and John had Paul take a third bottle and a small jar of ointment of which they were unsure, just to be safe.

"Master Barnwell said that she has had brief spells in the past, and that he was sure these tinctures have been beneficial, but this time the spell is much worse, and he thinks that she may need her priest at her side to pray for her recovery," said Paul in a worried tone.

As John locked up and they were pulling on their boots, he said, "I pray also that those tonics and the priest will help. Mistress Jane has always been so frail—like that filigree cross in the church." The pair trudged back up the road until they drew even with The Bell tavern and John pointed Paul to the vicar's cottage which was the last in the row before the churchyard. "Please tell Mister Barnwell that I wish the Mistress soon becomes well and that I will pass on the news to both of her sisters. I believe the Shakespeares were planning on traveling to Kenilworth to see the queen, and this may hasten their journey."

"I will, John, and thank you again for your help," said Paul. He had advanced several steps when he stopped and turned back. "Oh, I almost forgot. Master Barnwell said that this was written for Master William Shakespeare by his wife yesterday, and he wanted me to get it to the lad for her." Paul extracted a folded piece of paper from his vest pocket and handed it to John.

Ron could make out "For Will" written in a delicate scroll on the outside. "I shall see that he gets it," replied John, tucking it into a pocket and wishing Paul a safe journey.

Chapter 23.

JOHN QUICKENED his pace as much as possible given the conditions and had soon pulled the cart across the bridge and turned on the road to the right in the apparent direction of Stratford. Ron knew that William Shakespeare's father was John and his mother, Mary. *So that means that Mary has two sisters—one married to Mister Barnwell, that would be Mistress Jane, and another living in a town called Wilmcote, and her name is, what was it? Oh, Mary Margaret.* Ron found himself simultaneously worried about Will's aunt and anxious to see Will again, now that he was positive of the boy's identity.

The narrow, rutted road mainly tracked the course of the Avon upstream with the river on the right and hedgerows, fields, and stretches of thickets to the left. The traffic seemed busy on the road, and John often needed to pull off to the side to allow horse-drawn carts and carriages to pass around him. Except for low spots, the road was drying quickly, and there were many places where John could walk along the edge on the grass to avoid the muddier sections. After about a half-hour, John rounded a bend and then set his cart down just before a stretch where the road passed through a narrow thicket that ran down a small hill from the left to meet the Avon on the right. He pulled the stopper out of his sack of beer, took a healthy drink, and then stood on the grassy slope of the riverbank, staring for a time at the languid flow some ten feet below him.

John noticed something and tilted his head to the left, raising it at the same time and breathing deeply. He turned uphill and sniffed the air several more times.

His nose is a lot better than mine, thought Ron. And then, *Oh, right. It is his nose, after all.* He knew that John had picked up a scent that made him curious.

"Just to check on that fire," John muttered to himself as he crossed the road and hiked up the low hill along the side of the thicket. He, and thus Ron, could both soon see the thin blue line of smoke rising where the brush came to an end at the top of the rise. He moved more cautiously now and kept close to the damp bushes as he neared the source. It was obviously a campsite, with two lean-tos fashioned against a pair of small trees and a campfire which lay smoldering in the center. There was no sign of occupants, and aside from some oilcloth sacks, chipped pottery, one iron pot, and two piles of soaked rags, the area was empty. "Nope, nothing of bother," John said in a low voice as he then trudged and slid back down the slope to reach his cart and continue the journey to Stratford.

Activity picked up as their route left the riverbank and they neared the town. Houses had appeared on both sides of the roadway when Ron could make out a church spire further off to the right. *So, this is Stratford-upon-Avon,* thought Ron as they passed the church, expecting more of the town to unfold before him. *Or, not,* he realized minutes later as the houses petered out and they were once again following the river past open fields.

After another 15 minutes, Ron was certain they were approaching Stratford. Many more houses and a much taller church tower were soon apparent, and the closer they came, the busier the streets, the fancier the houses, and the more crowded the shops. It was soon apparent that they were in a town many times larger than John's village of Welford.

Ron found himself wondering whether John would choose to visit Simon first and deliver the wheel, or to bring the troubling news to Mary Shakespeare concerning her sister. John maneuvered the cart next to the wall of a two-story whitewashed timber framed house and set the handles on the ground. He reached for his leather bag and took a few swallows of his weak beer, straightened his clothes and hair, and then went up to the main door. He lifted and released the heavy knocker twice and waited. The door was pulled open by a woman with a baby on her hip and two small toddlers holding onto her skirts. "Yes, can I help you?" she asked, and then, "Oh, John, isn't it? What brings you here?"

"Hello, Mistress Shakespeare," said John. "Mister Barnwell has asked me to stop by and bring you word."

"Oh, yes? What word is that?"

"Well, it seems that your sister has… Well, she is doing very poorly at the moment."

"Oh, no! How badly does she fare? She is ill?" she asked with a sudden frown and a tightening of her hold on her baby.

"Yes, Ma'am," replied John. "Your sister is recently in Kenilworth. A messenger said that Mister Barnwell has asked me to tell you that they have been unable to rouse Mistress Jane, though they have tried to do so all through last night and into this morning. The rider was sent to fetch our priest and some of her things from their home in Welford. The messenger says that Mister Barnwell will send word once they know what the cause may be and asks that you may hasten your way to Kenilworth as soon as you are able."

Mistress Shakespeare sagged her shoulders as if the weight of the child was suddenly unbearable and said in a low voice, "Jane, dearest. She has always been a sprig of a thing, and any little breeze can knock her over. I hope this is not some ague."

"No, Ma'am. She has no fever says Mister Barnwell. She is fluttering her eyes, but cannot be roused. Oh, and you should know that she collapsed at our Welford wake two days past. But she was better yesterday when she travelled to Kenilworth," he added.

Now Mistress Shakespeare nodded her head. "She has suffered with mild fits since she was a child, and I remember one time when she was ten where she slept for an entire day for no reason at all. Let us pray that is all this illness is."

So, it's probably a form of epilepsy, guessed Ron as John stared at the ground.

"I must get word to our sister, Mary Margaret," said Mistress Shakespeare.

"No, no, that is all right," reassured John, seemingly glad to have a reason to raise his head. "I promised the messenger that I would go there myself and tell her once I've finished my business here in town."

"If you are sure, John? I can send her word from here."

"No, Ma'am, I made a promise, and it is easily kept."

"Thank you, John. I am so anxious about my sister now and must arrange for us to leave tomorrow for Kenilworth. And please stop back when you return from Wilmcote. Will would be so happy to see you. He'll be home from school later, and he said he enjoyed visiting with you in Welford."

"I shall, Mistress Shakespeare, I shall," said John, and Ron could hear Mary Shakespeare calling for someone inside the house as she ushered the children in and closed the door.

Don't forget the note for Will that the rider gave you! Ron shouted—uselessly. But, taking no heed anyway, John seemed more rushed now and soon had the cart back on the street heading the way they had come, retracing his

156

steps for several blocks before turning away from the direction of the river for another block.

While John made his way to the Penworthy house, Ron realized that he had passed through the stages of disbelief, despair, denial, and arrived at acceptance in his time with John—but not entirely so. He was also aware that one of his most frequent emotions lately was frustration. *I thought that when you died—if that's what has happened to me—that you simply dissolved into the ether. So simple. So liberating. So much for that idea...*

Then, as was his mind's habit, the sketch of a verse came to mind.

> Nothing's more solid than the ether.
> It pins me to a chipped cork notice board
> Next to the crooked Employee of the Month award
> And leaves me hanging below
> The unmoving hands splayed out on a clock
> In a bankrupt company's breakroom.
> This vacuous air is never empty but
> Filled with billions of flowing neutrinos
> Each invisibly poking me to stay where I am
> Glued to this paper-thin excuse for a world

John stopped before a house similar in many respects to the Shakespeare's in the front, but with attached wings jutting away from the street at each end. The section on the right held a small stable, and John angled the cart around it until they were in a courtyard where rested a three-wheeled carriage with an axle perched on blocks. A stableboy ran into the house upon his arrival, and a few moments later, Simon emerged.

"Greetings, John," said Simon. "I'm glad to see that the wheel is finished." He walked over to the cart and examined the replacement. "It looks like fine work as usual."

"Thank you, Simon. Yes, it should serve you well for years to come."

"Master Penworthy will be happy to be able to travel again. He is even threatening that he may be up for a trip to Kenilworth after all."

Ron could feel John smiling at the long face which Simon pulled as he said it.

"Well, at least you will not need to carry him," said John, bringing a chuckle to the both of them.

"This shouldn't take long," said John, "if you have another hand or two to help, that is."

"Yes, we do," said Simon giving a whistle. The stable-boy and a staff member from the house came out and stood beside Simon.

John reached into his tray of tools and brought out the mallet. He walked over and set it on the footstep of the carriage near the protruding axle and then returned to the back of his handcart.

"If you three could lift the carriage when I get the wheel there, I can slide it onto the axle without too much difficulty."

The three surrounded the sagging quarter of the carriage as John reached into the cart and wrested the wheel from its place in the back. Again, he held the wheel against his chest as he duckwalked to the side of the carriage and set it down for a moment. "Ready?" he asked. Three heads nodded, and then the men hoisted the carriage so that the axle was level while John lifted the wheel and after a little motioning with his head for the others to raise the carriage a bit more, he had it in place. They were about to set it down when John said, "No, a while longer." He grabbed the mallet and drove it hard against the hub to make sure it was well seated and then nodded for them to let the carriage down. He found two wedges that had been set in the back of the carriage and then used them to secure the wheel keeper in place.

"There you are, all done," he said. He reached over and gave the blocks which had been holding the axle off the ground a push so that they tumbled out of the path of the wheels. "Let's give her a try to make sure it stays true." The three men went to the front and raised the tongue, pulling the carriage forward while John walked backward in front of the wheel to gauge how it rode. "All right," he said after the wheel had turned a few revolutions. "It looks fine to me."

Simon remained with John while the other two returned to the stable and the house, respectively. "Master Penworthy would like you to have lunch in the kitchen, and we can make our payment there," said Simon.

"Thank you much, Simon, but I must hike now to Wilmcote on some urgent business."

"Oh? Do you mind if I ask the nature of it?"

"Not at all. It seems that Mistress Jane Barnwell from Welford has fallen ill. She had travelled with her husband to Kenilworth yesterday and was unable to be roused this very morning. Her husband wishes me to take word to her sister in Wilmcote. He is most anxious about his wife, as is her sister, Mistress Shakespeare."

"Master Penworthy must hear of this," said Simon. "He is a good friend of the Shakespeare's and is well acquainted with Mistress Jane. I insist that you come and have some stew while I arrange your payment and discuss this with my Master."

John nodded and followed Simon through a side door from the courtyard into the kitchen where the cook was already setting out a bowl of mutton stew with large slices of white bread. Ron could hear and vaguely feel the rumblings of John's stomach and so was not surprised when, despite John's earlier protestations, he immediately dug into the stew with many compliments to the cook. Simon returned mid-meal and joined John with a bowl of his own.

"John, here is your payment," said Simon, reaching across the table and dropping several large coins into John's palm.

"Very generous of you," said John, placing the coins in his pocket. "You must thank Master Penworthy again for me."

"That I will. Now, about Mistress Jane. My Master has directed me to ready the very carriage we just repaired, and I am to take you to Wilmcote. It will speed your journey and give us a chance to try out the new wheel. The horses have not been properly exercised for days."

"Thank you, Simon, I will gladly accept the transport. I can easily make the journey, but it will save much time, indeed."

"It is settled then," said Simon. "We will leave as soon as we finish our meal." He then turned to an adjoining chamber. "David! Tell Samuel to ready the carriage, and you help him as well."

"Sir!" came the short reply.

Finally, John gets to ride somewhere, thought Ron. He felt as exhausted as the man must be, and yet had done none of the actual walking himself.

Chapter 24.

As the carriage set out and they left Stratford, Ron found himself wishing that Sara was with him to take in this beautiful English countryside. They'd planned a trip to the British Isles, and now Ron had an intense desire to bring her to this very spot if he ever returned to the 21st century. *I'd give anything to see her again,* thought Ron. And then, upon further reflection, *In fact, I'd give anything to have my old life back. To write again. Hell, I'd even be happy to write another damn query letter... Or, even... screw stage fright—to talk in front of a roomful of people I don't know concerning a subject I know absolutely nothing about if I have to.*

Meanwhile, John and Simon were discussing sheep and crops as they passed through the broad, open fields—some filled with ewes and new-born lambs, and some being tilled for the spring plantings. Ron had trouble gauging the distance they travelled, but guessed that the walk there would take at least three or four times as long, and it seemed to be at the end of about a half-hour ride when they arrived at the few dwellings that comprised the hamlet of Wilmcote.

They were all three of them surprised when a woman came scurrying out of the large cottage they'd stopped before, saying, "There's something wrong with my sister, isn't there? What is it?"

John had thrown his eyes open wide, Ron feeling like he had done the same, and both John and Simon exchanged a quick glance. "Yes, there is," said Simon. "But how did you know?"

"I had a dream last night. I was with my sisters in a glen when one of them, my sister Jane, suddenly disappeared. We searched and searched for her, but she was not to be found. I awoke in a sweat thinking about it. It seemed so real that I've been anxious all morning. What has happened?"

The hairs on John's arms and neck had risen on hearing this, and he stuttered some when he first spoke. "M.. Mistress, a... a messenger sent from Kenilworth by Mister Barnwell arrived in Welford this morning. He, he says that your sister fainted last night and has been unable to be roused since. They are bringing the priest from Welford to help her, but her husband is worried about her. Your sister, Mistress Mary, was planning to travel to the celebration to see the Queen anyway, and Mister Barnwell has bid you both to come quickly if you are coming."

"But no fever? No other signs of illness?"

"No, Ma'am, not that we are aware."

Mary Margaret released the apron she had been grasping so tightly and nodded her head in a knowing manner. "Oh, then this is not completely unexpected. My sister has had spells since she was little—not to say that we shouldn't worry since they have gotten worse as she has grown older."

"So your sister said," replied John, "although Mister Barnwell seems more than concerned about this episode."

"Then I shall make arrangements to leave early for Kenilworth as well," said Mistress Mary Margaret. "Thank you for the message."

"Oh, I have forgotten to make introductions," said Simon. "John this is Mistress Mary Margaret Arden, and Mary Margaret, this is John Hart, who is Welford's—in fact, the region's—only wheelwright."

"Yes, I have heard of you John," said Mary Margaret. "Aren't you a cousin to our Jane's Peter Barnwell?"

"Why, yes I am," replied John. "It is nice to meet you, Mistress Mary Margaret, but I regret it is under unfortunate circumstances."

Mary Margaret nodded with a sober expression and bid them both good day as she turned back to the cottage.

❧

Once back in Stratford, Simon dropped John off in front of the Shakespeare's home. John bid him farewell and then knocked on the door which was opened immediately by Will. "Mister Hart! Hello! How does my Aunt Jane? Mother said you went to my other Auntie's to bring word there."

Ron mentally stretched out his hand, wanting to introduce himself. *It's a great pleasure to meet you, son*, he would have said, given the chance.

"No, no additional word yet on Mistress Jane, Master Will," said John. "I'm sure you will learn of her health before I do if you are going to Kenilworth."

"As we soon shall, I have heard," said Will, turning to face inside the house. "Mother! Mister Hart is back from Wilmcote!" he shouted.

There came an immediate loud "Shhhh!" which was followed by Mary Shakespeare's appearance at the door. "Will—the youngest are sleeping—please no shouting."

"I'm sorry, Mother, but you said that you wanted to hear when he returned."

"I did, son, but just not quite so loudly," she grinned, and then nodded to John. "Did Mary Margaret know anything more?"

"No," John replied. "She seemed to be of the same mind as you that this is a common ailment, but that it may be worse this time."

"It certainly sounds so—especially for Peter to request the presence of my sister's priest. I have sent word to my

John, and we are making ready to leave for Kenilworth tomorrow."

"That is probably wise, Ma'am."

"What are your plans now, John?"

"I am to return to Welford and await word from Mister Barnwell."

"Can I go with him, Mother?" asked Will. "I can be back by supper."

"No, William," replied his mother with an 'of course not' tone. "We need to begin packing and preparing for tomorrow's journey."

"But that will take no time. We can even arrange our things in the morning and still leave at a good hour."

Will is a procrastinator, just like me, thought Ron.

"William, the children are napping, but you could get the horse cart ready and see to the tack."

"Yes, Ma'am," he replied and then turned to John. "Have a safe journey, Mister Hart. I will be sure to tell you all about the Queen and the celebrations when I return home."

Don't leave! Ask to see his poems, John! Ron tried to shout. *Ask him to read you a poem! Oh, and you have a note to give him!*

"See you then, Master Will, and good journey to you tomorrow, Mistress Shakespeare." John bowed and then headed in the direction of Master Penworthy's house to retrieve his cart with Ron shaking his head inside John's head.

John had just turned his cart onto the main road to Welford and into the glare of the sun as it lowered to the west when he found someone walking beside him. "Master Will!" he exclaimed. "What are you doing here? Your mother meant for you to be busy at home."

"Oh, she is always doing things long before they need doing and fretting about things long before they need fretting. I thought I would walk with you part way. The day is too fine to waste in a shed."

"I must insist that you return home," tried John, "your mother will worry."

"And I must insist that I need a nice walk to breathe in the healthy vapors," retorted Will.

John seemed resigned to the wishes of young Master Shakespeare, and said, "All right, but only part way—only for a half-hour or so. Agreed?"

"Agreed!" Will said with a huge grin.

They had walked and chatted for five minutes when John suddenly stopped and dropped the cart handles in the middle of the road. Ron instinctively expected car horns to blare behind them.

"What is it?" asked Will as he watched John reach into his jersey and extract a rumpled piece of paper.

"I forgot to give this to you," said John, handing it to Will. "The messenger entrusted me with it this morning. It is from Mistress Jane. Mister Barnwell said that she wrote it for you the day they arrived in Kenilworth."

John picked up the cart handles and resumed pulling his much lighter load toward Welford while Will walked beside him, reading the note.

"She has given me another poem," breathed Will. "She writes: My Dear Will, we have had a pleasant ride to Kenilworth, and I watched the birds flying over the fields. This and the spring airs took my mind to when I was younger, and Mister Barnwell had begun to show his interest in me. I hope you enjoy it.

> Oh, I should like to fly up on a lark
> And with light wings write across the sky
> Words more beautiful than the sunset
> I see reflected in my true love's eyes
> On a lark, clasp hands and skip to town
> To do the things that lovers do
> Buy the girl a silken sash
> And let the gentleman begin to woo."

"Oh, a silken sash!" shouted John, giving Will a start. At Will's raised eyebrows he continued, "I have a list of things I promised to buy in Stratford, and completely forgot about it in all of the excitement! Thank goodness we haven't walked too far from town, Master Will. I need to turn back and make some purchases. Bother. This will take more time."

"Not too much," said Will. "I can do half, and I know all the merchants in town. What is it that you need?"

John repeated his rhyme, making certain to add the request of honey by Mrs. Allen at the end.

"Well done, Mister Hart, I never thought you were a poet, too!" laughed Will.

"Not hardly, young master, not hardly," grinned John.

Yeah, not hardly, thought Ron, having grown sick of the shopping list by this time.

The pair wheeled around and when they reached the market area, Will rushed off to procure the majority of the items. Really, all that John purchased were the oats and hops, but there was much dickering about the price and quality of the hops. Despite his short list, John was still later than Will whom he found loitering at the edge of the market with a small bundle of items and a mop when John caught up with him.

"All right, thank you Master Will. You have saved me so much time." Will plopped some coins in John's palm and stashed the bundle in the cart. "And you have saved me some money as well," said an appreciative John after counting the change Will had given him. He in turn placed two of the coins in Will's hand after some reluctance on the boy's part. "Now, I must insist that you head for home to help your poor mother out."

"But this trip to the market has taken no time at all and the sun is still high," said Will as the lengthening shadows said otherwise. "And, I have saved you in time and coins. I promise to turn back a little sooner than we had agreed."

"As you wish then, young Master, as you wish," said a resigned John.

This must have something to do with social status, thought Ron. *John is the adult here, after all, and his word should carry more weight.*

In much quicker time overall than Ron had expected, they were back at the spot where they had turned around. As if to replay the moment, Will took out the poem composed by Mistress Jane and read it aloud again.

"Ah, that is a fine poem," said John when Will had finished. "Another fine poem, indeed."

"Isn't it?" and Will held the paper in his hands, reading it over slowly one more time.

"How do they do it?" asked Will after they'd walked for a while.

"Do what, Master Will?" asked John.

"Poets. How do they write a poem? How do they find the right words?"

"Now, from what I hear from Mistress Jane, you are already quite the poet yourself, young Master."

John had his mouth open to continue when Will was momentarily distracted. "Oh, look! A bird's nest! I'm going to climb up and see if there are eggs, or if they are hatching. Walk ahead, and I'll catch up!"

John continued at a slower pace up the road while Will sought a good branch to begin his climb.

Ron thought about how he'd answer Will's question, and based on his furrowed brow, he guessed that John was doing the same thing.

Ron reckoned that he'd say something like this if he had the chance. *Well, Will, you take your time with the words and think about all that they can mean. Let's say that you want to describe a girl you like a lot, and you find her very pleasing to your eyes. So, she's a fair maiden. Then you think of a fair that is a fete with a juggle of clowns, and ribbons that rise in the wind, and everyone is happy and in awe. And then you might think of fair as justice where even a single fine hair on a scale can tip the balance either way. And then you think of your love, and you might write:*

> *She's a circus show rolled into town*
> *Smiles a spell across the land*
> *She flips her hair*
> *And just like that*
> *Other maids are whisps of air*
> *She's pitched her tent inside my heart*
> *Canvas flaps begin to dance*
> *A tightrope dare*
> *The watchers stamp*
> *Flags aflutter proclaim the fair*

Hey, he thought. *The Muse for that wasn't so bad after all. Where is a pencil or keyboard when I need one? All of this stuff is just going to disappear.*

Will came running up from behind with barely a pant. "There were eggs! Two! You should have seen them, Mister Hart—the bluest blue ever there was!"

"I bet they were, Master Will," said John, apparently still lost in thought. They walked on for a spell and the conversation turned to Mistress Jane. Will asked again about how people like her created poems as easily as they seemed to. Ron was desperate to weigh in, but, of course, had no outlet.

"I've been thinking about that, lad," said John. "I don't know about making the poems, but I watch their eyes and hear their sighs when people read them. They can strike as deep as a knife sometimes, and there's something there beyond the words." He paused a moment, having taken the matter in all seriousness. "I would say that you should keep living life the way you are, and the words will come. Keep looking for toads, climbing trees to see the robin's eggs, watching your brothers and sisters as they grow, listening to the grownups joke and laugh and argue. You just keep on taking it all in, and it will find its way back out. The poems are from people just like you, not the dolts like me, or the folks who brush and hurry past all that this great earth has to offer."

Ron was dumbfounded. His own explanation seemed like a mere platitude compared to this soulful observation. *Jeez,* he thought. *John's more of a poet at heart than I'll ever be. Maybe I can learn something from the old guy after all. Start paying attention to the basics instead of all of my abstract BS—living in my head . Which is, unfortunately, where I seem to be stuck right now...*

The pair, or the three of them, were about thirty minutes out of Stratford when they came to the spot in the road where a stretch of tangled bushes came down the hill, met the road, and even extended down the banks of the Avon on the other side. Ron recognized this as the place where John had walked up the hill to examine an abandoned campsite. The extent of brush was only twenty feet or so before they passed back to pastureland. Will was telling a story about two of his classmates and their encounter with a badger, but Ron could tell that John was distracted and getting nervous.

"Interesting, Master Will, very interesting," said John suddenly. "I'd love to hear more—especially what happened to that badger, but I'm fearing that you're far enough away from Stratford now, that you should be heading back, or I'll worry about you. I know your mother will have a fit if you're too late."

"But I thought I was going halfway," said Will. "I don't mind the walk."

"I know, but we'll see each other soon enough, and you can tell me about the Kenilworth festivities, Mistress Jane, and all the goings on there when you get back."

They were nearing a bend in the road when John stopped. Obviously to press his point, John set the cart handles down and tousled Will's hair.

In a flash, Ron saw this as his chance. His newly gained acceptance of his fate with John evaporated in an instant. As John's hand touched Will's head, Ron attempted to 'jump' over to Will . He had no idea how to accomplish this, but gave a valiant effort, nonetheless. He strained with all his might, but it was for naught. The brief moment had passed. He was crestfallen, but knew that he had had to try. He had realized that it would be some time, perhaps a very long while, before he saw William Shakespeare again and he was certain that he wasn't meant to be here with John, but rather with Will. Not with the illiterate, but with the true talent of the age. That was the only thing that made sense. What more could he learn from John?

"Are you sure you don't want the company?" asked Will, in a tone that showed he knew it was a hopeless question.

"Oh, I love the company, but the further we go, the bigger my worries will be about you making it home all in one piece, and I have a ways to go yet. Off you run, now lad."

Ron was still lamenting his failed attempt to join with Will when he noticed a bird whistle from the uphill side of the thicket behind them. *Now, that is the sickest sounding lark I've ever heard,* he thought. *Must be an English variety.*

"All right, Mister Hart, I'll see you soon," said Will reluctantly, but even so, turning around to head back home.

Then came a similar but more ragged whistle from the brambles on the water side. *That was no bird,* thought Ron. *That was a signal. I'm sure John heard it, too.*

John, however, appeared to be oblivious. He gave a wave to Will, picked up the cart handles, and started his way around the bend.

John! Shouted Ron. *That was a signal! It's the highwaymen! They're going to attack Will!*

No response. Ron was suddenly so frustrated that he pictured himself violently grabbing John around the throat and shaking him. Oddly, John stopped in his tracks and raised a hand to his neck, looking down as if lost in thought. He shrugged and took a few more steps in the direction of Welford.

Ron felt himself vibrating to the core and exploded. *John! TURN AROUND!*

John stopped again, hesitated, and then dropped the handles to reach into the cart. He had taken up the mallet, looked at it for a moment as if unsure, but was heading back around the bend when there came a stifled yelp from Will.

Thank God! thought Ron as John began loping as quietly as he could manage toward the boy's two attackers at the far end of the thicket. They both had their backs turned away from John and were manhandling Will, each grabbing a wrist—one stuffing a rag into Will's mouth, and the other holding a knife at the ready.

John chose the larger of the two when he reached them and drove his mallet down between his shoulder blades. The man crumpled at his feet, dropping his knife. Ron saw that poor Will had a look of absolute terror on his face. John kicked the knife into the tall grass beside the road. He wrenched the slighter man's hand loose of Will's arm and then dropped it to let the man face him. Without moving his eyes from the second man, John said, "You run home now, Will. And I mean run. I'll be able to handle these two." A quick glance from him was all Will needed. He spat out the rag and was off like a shot.

John let the smaller man land two soft punches to his face and then straightened his arm right into the poor man's nose. Ron heard the crunch, and then saw the sudden red results. John reached for the man's pants and his shirt, gathered these up in his fists, and then with two steps slung him out, over the bank, and into the river Avon. There was thrashing and sputtering from below as John checked and Ron saw that Will was already out of sight around a bend. John reached down for his mallet that should be near the first man, but it and the man were missing. He turned just in time to see the mallet heading for his temple and twisted away quickly enough to receive only a glancing blow. He squared with the attacker and gave him the same as he'd given the other, but this one was a little tougher. Blood streaming down his face, the bigger man suddenly stepped in close and rounded with the mallet. *Watch it!* yelled Ron, as John stepped back, but it was not enough, and he took the mallet full on his jaw. The world went black for both he and Ron.

Part III
An Unsolicited Review

Chapter 25.

RON WAS aware of a whistling in his head and the feeling that John's body had gone numb—frozen from the blow. He heard a strange otherworldly moan, and thought, *Uh, oh. John must be in a really bad way to make a sound like that. I have no idea what a death moan sounds like, but I hope to hell that wasn't it!* He was suddenly unsure if he could feel John's heart beating. He felt a rising tide of panic, but had nowhere to turn. *What happens to us if John dies?*

After stilling his thoughts for a few moments to calm himself, Ron reflexively tried to open his eyes as he had so many times in the past while John lay asleep. To his utter surprise, his eyes obeyed his command and he found himself staring at a night sky with a nearly full moon on display. Dazed, he watched as some lights of his eye's own making swirled about and gradually faded away. His brain was still stunned, but his body was responding. He blinked a few times and his eyes continued to do his bidding, focusing now on the constellation Orion shining prominently before him. He became aware of the cold gusts that buffeted him. *What?* he thought. And then "What?" he tried to ask aloud, hearing the word fade away with the screaming wind. "Yes!" he shouted with all his might. "I'm back!"

He found that his fingers were mostly frozen, so he rolled over onto his elbows and knees to stand up, however, a nearby small patch of crusted snow caught his eye, and he crawled over to it. With numb hands he scooped up what he could of the snow and rubbed the small rough chunks onto his face. He wanted to make sure that he was really and truly there and awake. To his delight, he found that he was.

He made it to his feet and retrieved his gloves, walking slowly downwind to retrieve each of them in turn. He walked several steps in the direction of home, but then stopped, letting the gusts try their best to topple him. Donning his gloves with numb fingers was a struggle, but with some help from his teeth, he managed it.

What just happened? he wondered. *Was that all only a dream?* The expanse of Lake Mendota and the bright lights from houses along the shore seemed to solidify his presence in twenty-first century Madison. *What happened to John? Did he die back there? Oh, my God.* Ron suddenly thought. *Is John in me now?* He tried with all his might to see if he could pick up some sense of the man's presence, but felt nothing. "John," Ron suddenly muttered in a low voice. "If you're there, don't panic. You're in… You're across the sea. You're in the New World, America, in a town called Madison, in the State of Wisconsin. You are also in the future by about four centuries. I'll never know if you are there, but if you are—good luck. Oh, and don't judge me too harshly."

Ron reveled in the immediacy of his senses and in the complete control he had of his surroundings. He swung his arms in big circles to get the blood flowing through his fingers again. He twirled about until he was dizzy. He ran and then dropped and skidded across the ice on his knees for the short distance the cold allowed. He hopped about on patches of snow to watch them break up and blow away. He marveled at the roar of a jet passing overhead on its approach to the Dane County airport and at the sudden blaring of a distant car horn.

And Sara! he suddenly remembered as he neared the shore and Tenney Park. *I thought I'd never see her again!*

Once ashore, he ran along the sidewalk and waved at a passing car with windows so frosted that he was amazed the driver could even see out. He suddenly realized that he must look like Jimmy Stewart running home in *It's a Wonderful Life.*

Ron stood in front of their house for a moment and stretched his arms wide, as if to hug the structure, and then bounced up the three steps to the front porch. He had a huge smile on his face while pushing open the front door, knowing that Sara should be home from work.

"Hi, Babe!" he shouted when the door swung open. There was no reply. There was no Sara.

"Sara?" he called as he stripped off his parka, gloves, and boots feeling the incredible warmth of luscious interior home heating flood his body. Noticing her coat on the rack, he called again, "Honey, I'm home!" And there was still no reply.

"Hey, Buddy!" said Ron when Cocoa came around the corner with a meow and rubbed his calf. "Where's your mom? Is she upstairs?" as he scooped up the cat and hugged him tight, eliciting a high-pitched squeak. "It's good to see you, too, Cocoa! Sara?" as he slid into his slippers.

"Where's your..." Ron addressed his cat, stopping in midsentence when he noticed the light glint off several drops at the base of the stairs. It was blood—distinct drops and some drying red smears that radiated out from them. Ron dropped the cat, looked up the staircase, and then back at the blood. *Where did all this come from?* as he noticed that a trail of drops led away from the base of the stairs.

"Sara!" he shouted, following the path of drying spots to the little TV room.

He found Sara passed out on the sofa, with a bad cut across the bridge of her nose and a nasty scrape on her forehead. There was blood on her sweater but not as much on her face as he might have expected. "Oh, Honey, what happened?" he asked as he momentarily cupped her head in his hands. She was warm and breathing, but it took several gentle shakes of her shoulders before she edged her eyes open. They darted back and forth a few times, and then Sara suddenly turned to the side and retched over the edge of the couch, narrowly missing his slippered feet.

Ron patted her back as Sara gasped for breath afterwards. "Sara, are you OK? What happened?"

"Ron?" Sara asked, closing her eyes, and lying on her back once again. "I don't know. I..." She suddenly knit her brows as if concentrating. "I was coming down the stairs, and then... I think I tripped on Cocoa. I woke up on the floor, stood up, and the world went dizzy after that. My knees buckled and then I crawled in here to lie down."

"I think we'd better get you to the ER, Hon. I think you might have a concussion."

"No, don't be ridiculous..." began Sara.

"Sara, do you open your eyes and then throw up on a daily basis?" Ron interrupted.

Sara thought for a moment and then gave a weak smile. "I'd better go get checked out," she agreed.

"I'm going to start the car to get it warmed up, and then I'll come back and clean a little before we go," Ron said as he gave her a gentle pat on the shoulder. "But first, a wet cloth to wash your face." He ran upstairs to moisten a facecloth, and was surprised to find a damp, bloody one already draped on the edge of the sink. *That's odd,* he thought, but put it out of his mind as he prepped Sara for the ride to the hospital.

Chapter 26.

SARA WAS situated next to him in the car with a bowl between her knees in the event that the nausea returned, but she had the window beside her cracked and the cold draft seemed to help keep the dizziness at bay.

Ron suddenly felt compelled to ask, "Were you in England?"

"What?"

"When you were passed out after you fell—were you in England?"

"Ron, what the hell kind of question is that? I was in La La Land if that's what you mean. I don't remember a thing. Why?"

"Oh, no reason," said Ron as they lapsed into silence for the remainder of the short drive to the ER. *That would have been something,* thought Ron. *Both of us passed out and in Elizabethan England at the same time. But that would be impossible. Everything that took place since I slipped on the ice was part of a dream. And yet, it all seemed so real...* and his train of thought ended as they pulled up to the ER entrance.

❧

It was like Old Home Week the moment they passed through the hospital doors. Sara, of course, knew everyone there and was embarrassed to find herself on the receiving end of treatment. Ron joined her in the blue curtain-defined cubicle after Sara was admitted and while her vital signs were checked, but he told her he would be in the cafeteria when they took her away for X-rays and an MRI, knowing that he would have a long wait.

He wished that they served beer—he suddenly had a hankering for a warm ale—but settled instead for a small silver pot of herbal tea, knowing that a cup of coffee at this hour would keep him up all night. After his tea had steeped and while he sipped at the mainly cinnamon-flavored concoction, he found himself again worrying about John. *That was quite a blow, and it knocked us both out. I hope John made it through OK. He's really pretty tough, but life was short back then. Too short. Ah, man, I hope the poor guy made it. How can I get back there? How can I check on him? And what about Mistress Jane? Did she recover from her seizure?* He reached for his phone, but realized that he'd left it at home in the rush to bring Sara here, and resolved to see what he could find out about them on the internet as soon as he had a chance to do so. Then his thoughts returned to Sara. *So, Sara and I were both knocked out at about the same time. I think I was out of it for just a few minutes at the most on the lake, but it seems like she was passed out for much longer. If I was with John in England during my few minutes, where was she, and for how long? Same time and place? And what a coincidence that both she and John fell down a flight of stairs.*

He finished his cup of tea and gave an inward chuckle at what was the most probable explanation. *But the sanest answer is, mine was just a dream and she really was in La La Land.*

Ron was amazed when Sara was wheeled over to the side of his cafeteria table in record time. Her face had better medical attention, and she had a Steri-Strip across the bridge of her nose along with a large patch of gauze on her forehead.

"Hey, how are you doing?" asked Ron. "What's the verdict?

"I'm OK," said Sara. "I have a mild concussion and nothing life-threatening. They gave me a prescription for the nausea and said I should take it easy for the next week—mainly sitting or lying around, or easy walks—but not on the icy streets. They don't want another fall to compound this. They wanted to have someone come by to evaluate our house for risk of falls, but I refused, and never told them about Cocoa. And they want me to stay on top of some anti-inflammatories. I might have some vertigo for a week or two, but I know the exercise to take care of that if it gets too bad."

She stared blankly at his teacup and appeared already drained by the conversation. But then she gave a heavy sigh, and Ron knew that there was more.

"What is it, Sara?"

"Well, I guess this ruins Christmas. I'm not able to drive; I can't help my folks with too much of anything if I was there; and you need to catch up on your website anyway. I'll call my folks tomorrow morning and give them the news."

"Oh, no you won't," declared Ron. "I'll finish packing for the both of us tomorrow morning, and we can leave in the afternoon. You need to be with your parents at this time of year, and I want to be there with you. Who knows how many holidays they have left in them, anyway?"

"Ron?" asked Sara. "Are you sure it was me whose head hit the floor?"

"Oh, you don't know the half of it, Sara. I was knocked silly, too."

"I was kidding," she looked at him seriously. "What do you mean?"

"Feel this," and he took her hand and held it to the lump on the back of his head.

"What happened?" asked Sara.

"Oh, nothing - slipped on the ice. I'll tell you about it when you're feeling a little better. Let's get you out of here."

The slow, iffy return ride with Sara sticking her head out of the window in sub-freezing air convinced her that she needed at least another day at home before she could handle the two-hour drive to Galena.

"Whatever you want, Hon, but I think the sooner the better."

Ron tucked Sara into bed, with Cocoa happy to join her under the covers. Switching off the light and closing the bedroom door, he found that he was starving and went down to the kitchen to fix himself a late snack, taking great care on the stairs on his way there. *But first things first,* he thought as he sidestepped the now-dried patches of blood on the bamboo floor. Grabbing some supplies from under the sink, he cleaned up both the blood and any remains from Sara's being sick in the TV room.

Back in the kitchen, he pulled open the refrigerator door, but was unexpectedly overwhelmed and pushed it shut again. He stood in the middle of the kitchen and felt overcome with gratitude for all that he, that they, had. Everything necessary, everything comfortable, everything unnecessary, everything uncomfortable. He was grateful for it all.

Reaching back into the fridge, he gently took an egg and thanked it for being there and for all that had made it possible for this egg to be in his house in a large city in the middle of a Wisconsin winter. Then he set about making it into the best, most flavorful egg sandwich he'd ever eaten.

Sated and tired, Ron decided it was time to turn off the lights and head for bed. He was about to rise from the kitchen table when he glanced at the window ledge and noticed the scrap of paper on which he'd earlier written the haiku about a morning drumroll. *Ah, I'd forgotten about that,* he thought as he set his dishes in the sink and then picked up and flattened the paper out on the countertop to reread it. But what was written there was not what he'd expected. Sketched in flowing lines were some wispy cirrus clouds, what looked like a willow tree to one side, a grassy hill that rose behind, and in the sky, a swirling line that led to a small bird in flight. He knew that Sara would have needed months of art lessons to draw this and wondered who had sketched it. Perhaps a friend of hers had visited and created the little image, because he had never seen it before.

He turned the paper over, and in the same flowing hand was written in large letters: *For Will, I feel I may be here for a long time, but this is in hope we might meet again.* Then this poem titled, *What is the Happiest Month?* followed below it, written over and around the haiku that he'd jotted down:

> Tis June with its easy warmth and greening lull.
> The joy of lamb and calf, piglet and foal.
> The leaps of corn and rye, of cabbage and kale.
> The tender grass bends as though it were a sail
> Under gentle winds that lightly kiss the cheek
> It lingers, and I am wrapped now in its eighth week.

Ron felt like he was momentarily transported back to Welford when he had met Will and they had read Mistress Jane's poem. The handwriting looked exactly the same. *How can this be?* he was gobsmacked. *Who could have written this? Sara? Is this some kind of prank?* Ron shook his head and flipped the page from front to back several times, but this didn't help in providing an answer. He was about to run upstairs to wake Sara, show her the drawing and poem, and quiz her about her experience while knocked out cold, but decided it was best, for her sake, to wait till morning.

He was exhausted, but found that there were a few pressing questions that he might be able to resolve before collapsing. Firing up his computer, he soon located Welford-on-Avon, along with Stratford-upon-Avon, Henley, and Kenilworth on Google Maps. Zooming in with the satellite view, he could find little that looked familiar from what he had experienced, except for the churches or cathedrals he had seen and the stone bridge leading out of Welford. And the now-famous house of William Shakespeare.

Once oriented geographically, he spent an hour trying to trace genealogical records, and was fairly certain that Jane Arden/Barnwell had survived her ordeal and lived until 1597. The names were spelled somewhat differently, and the dates seemed to be off from what he guessed they should be but, to Ron's great relief, it appeared that John had also lived through his encounter with the thieves. A John Harte had married a Grace Jones in 1577, but this was the only mention of his gentle host that Ron could find.

Yawning, Ron logged into his blog site to check for activity before heading for bed. *Oh, great!* he thought with chagrin after a few seconds of scrolling. *I've been hacked.* Following where he had made his last entry there were pages of what looked like stream-of-consciousness blather written by some demented troll. He prayed that it wasn't some maniac's manifesto. Too worn out to face cleaning up his site and resetting his passwords, he logged off in disgust and shut down his desktop.

The soft, enveloping bedding and mattress warmed by Sara soon had him dropping into a deep, dreamless sleep.

Chapter 27.

RON AWOKE to darkness, but felt refreshed. He was about to turn over and try to go back to sleep, given the apparently early hour, but then remembered that he was home in Madison, and it was winter. Checking the clock confirmed that it was 7:10 a.m. and he'd in fact slept in a little. He could hear Sara breathing deeply beside him and he lay on his back for a few minutes before waking her.

For some reason, the words about egotism from Nathan's poem, *Egotripping,* sprang to mind.

"While the rest squint through greasy goggles
For a glimpse of smeared smiles in the mirror."

Oddly, the wheelwright was simultaneously in his thoughts, and Ron felt slightly ashamed by the juxtaposition of the two. *I'm like one of those people in Nathan's verse—my self-image is totally distorted, and yet I can't take my eyes off it. I'm totally locked into my own ego. But as far as I can remember, John never did a single thing for himself—his whole life was dedicated to helping or serving others. Even his work seemed to be more focused on helping out the people who needed their wheels fixed than on making money. Is that how everyone was in England back then?* Images of the Webb brothers and recalling what he'd learned from Will about his own father quickly answered that question. *You know?* he asked himself. *I'd rather aspire to be a John than remain like I am.* Ron knew better than to make a resolution he might not be able to keep, but promised himself to try and change what he now saw as his own self-centered outlook.

Every poem I write is about what I feel, what I'm inspired to capture. But as soon as it's on paper or on my blog,

I obsess with the feedback and appreciation I might get. I can't let those go and just allow the poem to be the poem. I'm sure John never even thought about a wheel once it had been made. He was always on to the next that needed fixing. How can I have room for the new if I worry about those I wrote in the past? wondered Ron, becoming more appreciative of the time he'd spent with John.

Sara stirred. He reached over and gave her a gentle hug, and she took his arm and pulled it tighter against herself. "How are you feeling this morning?" he asked.

"Much better, I think." But turning over to face him, she suddenly said, "Ooh," while moving her hand up over her eyes. "Maybe not so great just yet."

"Would some coffee help?"

"Maybe, and an English muffin would help even more," she grinned.

Ron soon had her small breakfast in bed served, and Sara was able to sit up and eat—like she'd fasted for a week. Without much help from Ron, she was able to get dressed and make it downstairs—carefully—where she also consumed a bowl of granola with yogurt and berries followed by another cup of coffee. The only problems she had were in transitions—from sitting to standing, bending to upright, turning to the side. But while stationary or walking, she was fine. Ron helped her get comfortable in the TV room with her crossword, a book, and the remote.

Fixing breakfast for himself, he sat at the kitchen table staring out at the muted light from a slow dawn breaking outside. Still trying to piece together his experience, he walked himself through the steps he'd taken in his dream after falling on the ice during his Rite of Rejection. *And all of those poems are lost—the ones written by Mistress Jane, the one from the dream about the lady in the glass room, a poem that had something to do with Orion, and it's odd that I remembered that one written by Nathan.* It suddenly occurred to him that he couldn't recall ever reading the poem *Egotripping* except in his dream. Taking a last bite of egg-soaked toast, he carried his coffee mug to the book-cases and searched for Nathan's collection entitled *Steel Trees* with no success. *That was only in the dream, too?* he wondered. *I'm sure I remember having a copy. It had even won an award.* He then went through three other collections of Nathan's poetry, with no luck in locating the poem. Back in the kitchen, he decided to see if it was all in his head.

"Hi Nathan, this is Ron," he said when his friend answered.

"Hey, Ron, how are you? Are you in Galena?"

"Nope. Sara had a little accident, but we're going to head down there as soon as she's ready."

"Oh, no. Is she OK? What happened?"

"She's fine, and just resting up now. She tripped on the stairs last night and knocked her head. She has a mild concussion, but the doctors say that she's fine."

"Well, that's a relief! Tell her I hope she gets better soon. And tell Pete and Gladys that I wish them a Merry Christmas when you get there."

"Thanks, will do, Nathan. How was Hanukkah?"

"It was great. Now I'm looking forward to Christmas for all of the food and parties."

"Me, too. Say, the real reason I called is to ask you about a poem you maybe wrote."

"Yeah? Which one?"

"Well, this might seem a little odd, but I had this weird dream where I recalled a poem you'd written named *Egotripping* in one of your volumes titled *Steel Trees.* I looked for it again this morning and can't seem to find it. Did you write one with that title?"

"I'm flattered that you dreamt about me, Ron, but I never wrote a poem with that title, let alone the book. What was the poem about?"

"That is so bizarre. It was in your style and was loosely about how all of us wander around looking through greasy goggles into our own mirrors, and can't relate to those few of us who are able to escape our own egos."

"Great idea! Mind if I steal it?"

"Hey, as far as I knew, you wrote it in the first place," laughed Ron, at the same time wondering to himself just who had written that poem.

After some small talk, Nathan reinvited Ron to join him on his book signing tour.

"I'll have to check my schedule with Sara, but I think that might be a possibility," Ron said when Nathan had finished. This time he didn't immediately dismiss the offer out of hand.

He began to go through the motions of getting ready for work, but then remembered the disaster of their Holiday crunch, and that Crone Amplifiers wouldn't be picking things up again until the new year. Feeling somehow light and free, Ron was headed to the study when he remembered the state in which he'd found his blog the previous night, and his mood was brought back down to earth. He dreaded all of the work that cleaning up from the hack would entail, but before sitting at his computer, he wanted to reread the poem left by Mistress Jane and show it to Sara. *That's odd. Where did I put it?* he wondered as he leafed through the papers on his desk and searched in a few drawers for the poem she'd written for Will. *Wow, I must have really been tired last night,* he thought, now unsure whether it was the existence of the letter or where he had put it that was the cause of his inability to locate it. He retraced his steps through the house from the previous evening, even wondering if he'd brought the scrap of paper upstairs to bed with him, but could find no sign of the missing poem. Giving up for the moment, he poured himself another cup of coffee and then headed for his computer.

Once logged in, he navigated to the latest entries in his blog to peruse and then delete the crap the troll had left. Scrolling quickly down, he found that there were pages and pages of the rantings, and Ron reasoned that whoever the troll was had written them beforehand and had then uploaded or pasted them all as a single file—the volume was far too great to have been written while he was out on Lake Mendota.

He knew that he should just delete the entire batch and then set a new password immediately, but curiosity got the best of him. Steeling himself for what the worst of the content might hold in store, he began at the top of the new entries.

Chapter 28.

RON WAS shocked to see that the first post had been written by Sara.

Rn-TLC: I am better now. In the beginning I had the fierce pangs of panic. I wailed for the loved ones whom I had left behind. I keened with all my might in mourning, and I screamed aloud in angry fear. I had surely landed in Hell and the Devil was having his way with me. He had my soul and I had lost my mind.

What the heck is this? Sara panicked? Was it the fall down the stairs? wondered Ron. *Is she trying her hand at poetry?* Then, *Uh oh, I think it was Sara who was hacked— she's not the least bit religious.*

Rn-TLC: But then upon waking, it was as if a storm had passed, and now I am calm. I remember. I have been here before. I have not been to this place before, but I have been in this condition before, under the same spell. This is a strange, new world, and I am resigned to being here until this passes. It will not last. It soon will all be as it should. I am certain of this: I am having one of my episodes, and I will soon return back home.

This world is new, but the travelling is not. I have been to places with white marble and flowing gardens, of hide tents and hairy horned beasts, of tall trees and wooden boats on the sea, of tridents and tiered towers, with serpents and strangling vines, and of curved blades and fur hats. I have endured all of those places and I can survive this world.

No one suspects, and I will never disclose the lands I have visited during my spells upon my return. Oh, I have seen what happens to witches, and I am not a witch. People betrayed them; thus, I must never breathe a word lest others betray me. Two witches I saw hanged in Coventry when I was younger, and I learned of many more hanged or burned in London. There remain whispers of witches in every village everywhere.

Spells and witches? Wait a second! thought Ron. *This sounds like someone from the England that I just left! How could Sara possibly know about this—if she wrote it?*

Rn- TLC: But now the whispers are dying down like the embers of the fires that burned those poor souls. I must never speak of this, and I am not a witch. I know not what this illness is nor why these dreams become more than dreams, but I know that this shall pass.

At this, Ron found himself thinking, *The spells, or fits. Leaving behind loved ones. References to England... This seems so much like Mistress Jane. But that's impossible. Unless she was experiencing Sara's reality while I was living through John's? But the writings here don't seem to follow the same pattern. I couldn't control John in the slightest. Plus, Sara could never have logged into my blog and written this while she was passed out. And anyway, she wouldn't have had the time to write this even if she wasn't. It couldn't have been Sara—I don't think...* and he scrolled down so he could read more with a slight shiver up his back.

However, Ron couldn't stand not knowing, and pushed his chair away from the desk. Sara was propped up on several pillows working a crossword puzzle. She smiled at him as he came into the TV room and plonked himself down on a nearby chair. "How are you feeling, Hon?" he asked, out of genuine concern, but also to ease into the conversation. He gave the slightest grimace at the sight of her face. *Poor Sara*, he thought. A bump on her head and one on her nose had both swollen, and her eyes were ringed with dark purple.

"Much, much better. I got up to get some tea and had no vertigo. The only time it seems to happen now is when I lie back down. Then things get pretty spinny."

"Do you think you can handle the drive tomorrow?"

"Yep. I really think I can," replied Sara, immediately continuing with, "but I'm bringing a barf bag just in case."

Ron nodded. "Good idea." He fidgeted a bit, and then came to the point. "Say, Sara?" She looked over at him with eyebrows raised. "Do you remember when I asked if you had been to England after you fell down the stairs?"

"Yeah, what a strange thing to ask, Ron. Especially when I was so out of it."

"So, now that you're back to normal, do you have any memories of England at all? Anything?"

"No, why would I? Like I said, I have no memories of anything much," she paused, and Ron looked at her expectantly. "The only thing was this run-of-the-mill dream of being in our house and looking through a book of poetry. I never do that, and I don't even recall which one it was. But definitely nothing to do with England."

Ron remembered the washcloth in their bathroom the night Sara had fallen. "Honey, you said you were passed out on the couch the whole time, but I found a bloody washcloth on our bathroom sink, and your face wasn't smeared with that much blood. You had to have made it upstairs and cleaned up—do you remember that?"

"I did?" asked a perplexed Sara. "I don't remember that at all—or England—or anything."

"And it looks like at the same time that you were passed out, either you were hacked or you typed some entries on my blog—with all of these details that sound like they came from..." Ron paused and shook his head. "Okay," he started. "The reason I asked about England in the first place is because I just had the strangest... experience, or dream, or something." He then told her how he had fallen on the ice and then spent a couple of days in Elizabethan England within the life of a local wheelwright—even meeting a young William Shakespeare. Partway into the story, Sara sat up—slowly—leaned forward, and paid rapt attention until he finished.

"Ron, that is incredible. I mean, I have dreams, but yours are so vivid by comparison. You should really write this down. It makes a great story."

Ron slid out of the easy chair and moved to sit next to her. "It did occur to me to write it down. Maybe I will someday. But there are some parts that make this all a little stranger."

Sara snuggled close to him, and he put his arm around her shoulder. "I had never heard of Welford-on-Avon before, but I looked it up on a map, and it is an actual town downstream from Stratford-upon-Avon. On Google Earth, the stone church is exactly as it looked then."

"You're joking," said Sara.

"No. And I checked some genealogical records, and the people I met really existed. Well, the Shakespeare's of course, but the others too. John Harte married Grace Jones a few years after I was there."

"Shut the fuck up!" exclaimed Sara, giving him a shove in the ribs.

"No, I'm serious. And there's more."

Sara now slowly twisted to face him head-on. Ron looked at her for a minute and then asked. "Search your memory, Sara. Is there any chance at all that you have any recollections of where you were when you were out—besides that dream?"

She shook her head, but then squeezed her eyes shut and clenched her hands into fists for a moment before relaxing them and dropping them back on her lap. She opened her eyes slowly and Ron could see the pupils darting quickly back and forth. "Ooh, just a sec. I gotta lie down."

Ron rose from the couch and then helped her get situated against the pillows.

"Need the bowl? Some ice?"

"No, I'm OK, it's passed," said Sara. "I remember very little about being out cold, but I know I didn't dream anything other than what I told you about reading a poem. I know I was here, because I managed to pick myself up off the floor and make it onto this sofa. And I was aware of that the whole time. I think. Plus, I'm sure it happened not long before you got home."

"Do you remember I started to say that I thought you were hacked? You won't believe this, but right now I'm reading stuff that you posted on my blog. And everything you wrote sounds exactly like it was from Jane Barnwell's perspective. Not only that—she left a handwritten poem on a piece of paper in the kitchen."

Sara's eyes widened and then as quickly narrowed. She studied her partner with obvious skepticism. "Let's see it," was all she said.

"I'll look again, but I must have misplaced it last night. I'm sure I can find it. It was even addressed to Will."

The look of skepticism remained. "What about the blog?"

"I'm reading it right now. I'll print it or copy it into a file when I'm done and show you."

"Are you sure you weren't just hacked or something?"

"Nope, if anyone was hacked, it was you. Here, let me go get your laptop and we can check."

Ron was back in a minute and handed the computer to Sara. She logged in. "Everything seems fine," and then she frowned.

"What is it?"

"Well, it shows the most recent document I had open was named 'Document1,' but when I click on it, the message I get is 'can't be found.'"

"Does it show when it was saved?"

"Yeah… about the time you were gone, and I was out. That's just too creepy, Ron."

"I think you'd better run your antivirus software and change your password, Hon."

"I will, but that still doesn't explain who it was—and I highly doubt it was Mistress Jane. I mean, how could it be?" Sara then sighed and lowered the timbre of her voice. "Ron, are you sure this isn't all just a joke by Brendan? He's been doing this kind of thing since college and he could have somehow made it look like the post was from me to play a trick on you. It sounds just like ol' BL, doesn't it?"

"Actually, it does. But that idiot isn't that clever. He couldn't pull something like this off. Besides, how would he know to make the specific references to England?"

"Pick a theme, and BL is the expert and can beat it to death as you well know from your blog. Honestly, I don't know how, but I would look to your friends before I bought into it being a visitation from an Elizabethan damsel in distress."

Ron vividly recalled several elaborate pranks Brendan had played on various friends. When he realized that the poem written in flowing script could have been a late-night figment of his own tired imagination, his shoulders sagged. "You're probably right. I'm going to finish reading it, but with eyes wide open to any anachronisms or little nuggets that don't fit. Thanks, Hon."

Sara smiled back. "Well, if it really is her, I definitely want to read it," she said encouragingly.

"For sure," he said, with a little less confidence than he'd had before he'd talked with her. "Need anything while I'm here?"

"Only a kiss, you big romantic, you."

Ron leaned over and gave Sara a meaningful and lingering kiss. He made sure she was settled and then headed back to the study to pick up reading where he'd left off.

Rn-TLC: How do I know to do this? I have no names for some of these things, yet I can use them! The pen that flows with no inkwell, this alphabet—I push these letters and they mirror in the picture! The levers that bring light, the knobs that turn to open doors, the handles that bring water as from a fresh cool spring, the twists that bring fire to the kitchen—with no wood!

This world is light, and it is everywhere. Coming from within this picture frame—and not merely reflected off it! Every box I open seems to have light within. The street at night is bright, and each and every home has warm glorious light pouring out of the windows.

I know this is not heaven, but parts are heavenly indeed. I know not where I am, nor what year it may be here, but I do know that it is winter. I have stepped outside into the bitter cold night with its deep, old, packed snow, but inside the house is marvelous warmth—with no fire to make it so! Every room is the same climate and there is not a draft to be found while the wind yet howls and beats the walls outside.

I have observed. From inside this house, I can see carriages go by with no horses to pull them, nor men to push.

They hug the road and have the fattest wheels and piercing lights that shine only before them. I fear to go out, but it is so cold that I am content to remain inside for now, regardless. I know not whether there is a Spring in this world. I have left my favorite season when life prevails and all is green, and I have been plunged into the depths of winter. I pray that I may see a living thing again.

If she was here, I wonder why she doesn't mention Cocoa? wondered Ron. *She would surely notice him.*

I cannot begin to describe the strange marvels within this dwelling. The lights—again, the lights - globes with no flame—many cool to the touch as if filled with foxfire and fireflies. The box that is forever cold inside, and within it many strange and some marvelous foods. Vegetables fresh as just picked from the garden. In the midst of winter. So much food! The small box that is as frozen as the wasteland outside. The round tins with drawings in such detail that it is as if the very thing itself is there before you - and within the tins are those same things. I know this because I somehow used a device to open the tin with a beautiful drawing of beans - and those very beans were inside—already cooked! I have seen drawings of people so like in life that it is as if they were standing before me. I expected them to begin talking at any moment.

Ron jumped up, went into the kitchen, and rummaged through the recycle bin. There, near the top was an opened can of kidney beans. He held it for a moment, and then walked to the TV room with the can in his hand. "Hey, Sara? Did you open this can of beans?"

She looked up and nodded. "Yeah, remember the bean salad I made the other night? Why?"

Ron did remember the linguini and salad they'd had. "Oh, yeah. I forgot. Thanks," as he turned back to the kitchen.

"Why, Ron?" asked Sara behind him.

"Oh, nothing," said Ron as he returned to the bin and dug through it to see if there was another can of beans. He found four more - another can of kidney beans, one of cannellini, and two of garbanzo. *Oh, nothing, I'm just losing my mind,* he thought on the way back to the study, knowing opened cans of beans were no proof of anything.

Rn-TLC: Oh! And water! And polished silver! No one would ever dare drink the water in Welford unless they sought a painful illness.

Aha! thought Ron as he began reading again. *I know I'm right!*

Rn-TLC: And we would only chance to partake of that which was caught from the fresh springs off the road to Henley. But here the springs are inside the house! Such clear, pure water you never saw. Never tasted. My hands knew that with the push or pull on some lever it would flow. And that lever—the most polished, high-quality silver—like a looking glass! But here is the more Devilish part. Another lever brings water so hot that it can burn. Steam fills the basin. It is a mystery—and can I trust it? There is no smell of sulfur, and yet perhaps the Devil lurks.

And so, I have learned that not all of what I find here is pleasant. There is some evil about, or I am damned. There are nubs on the walls, and my hands knew that a push up brought light and a push down extinguished the flame. However, one lever in the kitchen produced such a growl from the basin that I leapt out of my skin and expected the very hounds of Hell to leap forth. There are milder hounds that reside in the privy room ceiling. I might avoid that room, but it is necessary. Not to be indelicate, I might add that the privy room is—words escape me. Luxurious? My body knew that the water-filled bowl was a chamber pot, and I used it as a lady might. Unexpectedly, a paper for cleanliness. A rush of water and all was as it had been. How is this possible? And the crystal-clear looking glasses upon the walls!

But whyever did I open that window of life? It haunts me now. I yearn to open it again, but it repels me at the same time. It is definitely the Devil's work. I looked through that window straight into the midst of other people's lives. Some are real and pleasing, some are too horrible to tell. Like the stuff of which nightmares are made. I have witnessed death and screamed at the sight of it—and then several more. Why must there be so much shouting, people showing me things they are excited about, things they hold right up to my face. They plead with me, but I cannot help them.

Ron sat back in his chair, staring at the screen. *It was Mistress Jane,* he thought. *It has to be. Maybe she was transported here while she was in the midst of her fit in Kenilworth. That must be it. But, how could she be here at the same time that Sara was in the house and not encounter her? Was she inside Sara? No, Sara claims not, and Mistress Jane's account of being here doesn't seem like it's the same thing that happened to me and John. I couldn't manipulate objects in the slightest, for one thing.*

He reached for his mouse and scrolled down. There were replies to what she had posted.

BL: Ron, who is this? I always thought that Rn-TLC was Sara. I don't get it. *Encino Woman* in your website? In your house?

Georgio: What a short story, Rn-TLC. Kind of like the opposite of *A Connecticut Yankee in King Arthur's Court*. But do you think Poetriter will be happy with you taking up all this space on his blog?

Malaprop: Makes me appreciate what I have. The language needs a little work, but great start.

BL: Ron, are you there? It's been a couple of hours. Have you been hacked? Only asking because you haven't responded. If it is you, you don't sound the same.

Georgio: I think that is kind of the point, BL.

BL: Stuff it, Georgio.

At the end of the comments, it looked like Mistress Jane, if that's who she was, didn't respond, but continued with another post.

Rn-TLC: I understand more now about what this is, and that it belongs to someone else. I have gone back and read the words he has written. It is like the diary of a person's thoughts and poetry. Meaning no disrespect to him, I feel that I must say my piece about his thoughts on writing.

Oh, Dearest Reader! Pay no heed to a word he has written about our craft! You live in a time that blesses your creations! The ease with which you can put thought to page and page to print is a gift to be treasured. An age in which all can be read and written without effort—you send words out with the press of a button! So many ways to create are here—along with the time and leisure to do so. This lighted picture frame has shown me instruments and instructions, paints and lessons, music and dance, words and courses—all to be had by any who desire. And desire you should! What is life without creation? Flood the world with it! There are volumes on his shelves alone. So many books, such a collection!

I read what he wrote about publishing and the futility of finding someone willing to undertake that endeavor. I am well acquainted with a time when all is hand-lettered and the printed word is only for the landed rich, the well-respected, and the Holy Bible. And now anyone can print with ease, and it is possible to publish a book by oneself.

Don't let the struggle in finding someone to publish what you have written quash your dreams. The books you print can sit proudly on your own shelves. They are not paper boats we set out on a lake, they are the petals of cherry blossoms, the summer insects, the autumn leaves that fall upon the waters—all the product of a bountiful summer's creation! We must set them out as the chicks must leave the nest, and clematis must put its seeds to the wind. Write! Publish!

What an age you live in! Is it better to have one million people and five books available, or five people and one million books to choose from? What if your work finds one reader! The quail may have one chick that survives the clutch, or the clouds of cottonwood fluff might make one tree. That is all that matters.

So, take Heart, precious Author! Do not think that the thoughts that inspire are for others alone. There is not one Muse, not one Divine Fount. No, there are endless streams, brooks, and springs to drink from and they will flow when you write! Do not think that the pump is seized or the water body frozen—the flow cannot be dammed, and the source is unending. Simply open up and write! The words will be there when you need them!

Let your reader touch your face, smell your breath, feel the anguish in your chest, taste your tears, and feel the spasms in your back as you laugh. Tell them how your eyes drink the sunset, how your ears harken to the stars, how your nose sniffs out your dreams.

There were some comments following this, but her sentiment had thrust Ron back to his experience in Welford. *Oh my God,* he thought. *What an ass I've been,* as he thought of John. *The guy could hardly read or write; there was not a scrap of paper or quill to be found. No written words except for some handbills on the tavern wall and Mistress Jane's small book collection. Nobody read. Only a few of the better-off wrote. And here I am telling people that writing and publishing are pointless, rather than more than worth the effort? How many writers have I turned away from trying?* He then remembered the extremely small, no, miniscule, following his blog had, and that this probably wasn't a huge thing to worry himself over. *Well, thank God for that. But have I even discouraged myself from appreciating the simple act of creation?*

Ron realized that he'd been a walking contradiction— railing against the publishing industry but desperate to be part of it; telling others it was a mistake to try while he himself couldn't quit writing. He turned back to Mistress Jane's post which had brought him up short. *And she certainly has quashed my image of my works disappearing across the lake only to be sunk by others. I think she's basically saying that our poems are the lake...*

Chapter 29.

SARA CALLED out from the TV room. Ron straightened himself up from his chair and automatically followed her voice, since his head was momentarily in a completely different dimension. "Hey, Hon," he said as he mustered at least these few words out of the space-time continuum.

"I was just wondering if you were thinking about lunch anytime soon, hint, hint?" she smiled at him.

Ron rubbed his scalp vigorously in an effort to focus. He then looked down at his watch. "Sure, it's looking to be about that time, isn't it? Hmm, how about veggie chili on toast with some sharp cheddar cheese melted on top?"

"Oh, that sounds divine, Ron—thanks!"

He smiled back and had started for the kitchen when she said, "Hey, Ron?" He stopped and turned. "I was just thinking that I'm feeling much better, and I really believe that I could manage a car ride. Any possibility that we could drive down to Galena this afternoon?"

Ron was silent for a moment, still thinking about what he'd been reading on his blog. Then he began nodding. "Yeah, Sara, we should be able to do that. I still need to finish packing, and I'm wrapping up—or trying to wrap my head around—the website, but if we leave mid-afternoon, we can easily make it there by dinnertime. Would your folks be all right with that?"

"I think so. I talked to them earlier, and they obviously understood why we couldn't come right away, but it was pretty clear they were disappointed by the delay. How about if I call them while you make lunch, and see what they say?"

"Sounds like a plan," said Ron and turned again for the kitchen.

Ron was surprised at how well lunch turned out, since he was still processing what he'd read, reconciling it with his experience in Welford, and with Sara's fall down the stairs here at home.

He carried their two plates out to the TV room and joined her over their sloppy lunch. "What did your folks say?" he asked between bites.

"They were ecstatic, of course, and Mom said she would make something for dinner that could be reheated in case we were a little late. I think going to any parties this holiday season is out though."

Funny, I was actually looking forward to them for a change, thought Ron, but he then asked, "Why is that?"

"Have you noticed my face? At all?" at the same time framing it with her hands in exaggerated horror.

"Ah," he said cooing, "I've been beginning to think of you as my little raccoon..."

She twisted to grab a pillow to throw at him, but the motion was too quick and vertigo stopped her short.

Sara took a moment and then smiled, "Just make sure you pack a paper bag for my head, will you?"

"Okie dokie," he said jokingly while taking her plate. And then more seriously, "I have a few hours left so I'm going to finish packing and then attack my website."

"Take no prisoners," she smirked as she took up her crossword and began tapping her pencil against her lips.

"Oh, and Sara?"

"Yeah?" she asked, looking up at him as he stood near the doorway, dishes in hand.

"Remember I said that I was in England, but experienced it all through another person, through John?"

She nodded.

"Well, I just wanted you to know that I'm now convinced that it was Mistress Jane who wrote on my blog under your alias. And I think that she was experiencing our house, our world, through you." He described what he had read so far.

"What?" Sara let the pencil drop onto the crossword. "That's nuts, Ron. Besides, I was passed out and didn't move from this spot."

"What about the washcloth with blood? The handwritten poem? Typing out the blog? She couldn't have done those things without you being the one to actually carry them out."

Sara gave a shiver, but said, "Don't be ridiculous. Remember you said that you had absolutely no control of anything when you were with John? And now you're telling me that I was possessed while I was passed out and zombied around the house accompanied by Mistress Jane? The two don't jibe at all. You can't have it both ways."

"Think of it from John's perspective. Maybe he fell down his stairs and was really blacked out the entire time I had that experience in England. Maybe he woke up at the bottom of the stairs after I left. Who knows?"

"Precisely! Who knows?"

"Look, I'm just trying to come up with an explanation, and that's the only way I can see that this fits. Either that, or you don't remember going upstairs but really did, and my website is possessed."

"But when, exactly, would I have had time to do all of what you described during that short time you were out on the lake? Come on, Ron. You might be overthinking this."

Ron considered her point for a moment and nodded. "Yeah, maybe. But just let me know if you have any ideas or remember anything else, OK?"

"Will do, Hon, will do," she said as she closed her eyes and lay back on the pillows, forehead wrinkled in concentration.

*

Ron put the dishes in the dishwasher and was eager to get the trip preparations out of the way. He went upstairs, packed for them both, and lugged the suitcases down to the front door. Everything seemed to be in order other than his blog, and he headed to the study to continue reading where he'd left off.

The replies following Mistress Jane's admonitions to never quit writing were varied.

> StanzaGuru: I salute you, Rn-TLC. I've held back on making any comments about Poetriter's diatribes concerning the publishing business, and his negative attitude toward the whole process, because I've always felt that the act of writing should be independent of the fate of the writing. Get down what you can while you can because who knows how long each of us has on this planet? There's nothing to wait for—go for it, in my opinion. If you have the time and energy for the pursuit of publishing, more power to you. I'm like Poetriter mentioned in one of his poems—I write my words on the wind and on the waves.

> Georgio: I agree with SG.

> BL: Who ARE you, Rn-TLC? What have you done with Ron?

> VisaVerser: I also agree with the poster and with StanzaGuru. I've been a lurker here, and have to say that I like Poetriter's poems, but always felt depressed by the rantings.

Then came a section from Mistress Jane that hurt as he read it, at least on the first pass.

Rn-TLC: I do not understand. This man says that he is a poet. Oh my, I hope that she is not a woman, for to think that a woman would write in such a way is just beyond my sensibilities.

However, assuming a man, he states that he is a poet, and yet I find no poetry in what he writes. I have read and thought and read again, and I still do not understand how he can make this claim. Of course, there are some subjects that are beyond my ken, but it is not solely the substance; it is also the form that matters. A poem must be structured, otherwise it is merely a collection of sentences. His lines are split at will, have little punctuation, little or no rhyme, so how can this be poetry? I will admit that the words he writes are beyond mere sentences, and perhaps that is what poetry has become here. I see internal rhyme, I see clever turns of phrase, I see unexpected connections, I see parallels, but I see no poetry.

How is this art—to not fit the verse into meter, to not have an ending rhyme, to simply spew words across the paper? There is no discipline. There is no fully formed description, no ornamentation. What is the point? It is as if a beautiful winding garden has restricted visitors to the central path far from where the gardener put in all of his work. The main message is apparent, but in such sparse wordings that we might as well have the skeleton of the pig for dinner rather than the luscious meat, which is the entire purpose of a roast pig, I might say.

This, by my meager skills, is what I have written to show where I believe poetry should start, although this is a paltry effort, but serves to sketch the form:

Reflections

Tot squats to see herself in the puddle
Stamps her feet and then a wrinkled face grins back.
The brook's calm, a pool reflecting Spring so subtle
A thin girl is tugged away with a laugh.

Slow strolls along the banks, but the stream's ignored.
Where others see two hearts, they know but one.
Focused on the mirror. He has implored
She become his bride, so much to be done.

Spilt milk, cracked plates, she startles at the sight
Of a fraught mother's stare in the mop's pail.
Goblet with etched vow is where dust alights
Dull reflection, has she become so frail?

The crone lies down, sees her face in the glass
Deepened wrinkles, how has this come to pass?

I have found this following work among the many
verses that were written by the owner of this collection. I
believe it is a good example of the undisciplined manner in
which he approaches his art.

I remember its smoke.
Winking one eye shut
As the cigarette dangled from his mouth,
Him leaning in under the open hood,
Hand out for a wrench.
Or the pulsing glow
While the wind burned it down to the filter
After he'd barely had a puff.

And when he flicked it out over the water
Hitting the surface to disappear with a pssst.
Letting me have my own to run off
And use it as a punk to light my firecrackers.
The slight crackle when he'd use the glowing dial
Of the car's pop-out plug for a light.
A line of gray ashes when he had the best intentions
But left in distraction.
It's sometimes difficult to picture his face, but
I remember my father by the smoke and the ash.

There is much in this that I do not understand, and I make the assumption that this 'cigarette' is a device for smoking tobacco—that smelly habit his father shares with my husband. However, I do see that he has described his relationship with his father using one constant image. That is perhaps this poem's essence. And perhaps that is the point in this place. Perhaps in this place, that is what poetry is—to reveal the essence.

I never realized until this moment that I always seem to visit the place of a poet during my spells. So, perhaps that means that this person is a poet after all. I try and practice the poet's art, although I cannot share what I write with more than a few. I think young William will become one. I believe that is his destiny.

Whoa! After all those put-downs she called me a poet! thought Ron, not sure whether to have that declaration outweigh all the dings his ego had taken at her hands. He continued scrolling down.

BL: Hey, Ron, I can see some self-criticism once in a while, but if this is you, this alter-ego crap is a little much. Even as an experiment, it ain't a'work'n.

Ron thought about clarifying the situation for his readers until he realized that the explanation would be more convoluted than just leaving things as they were. He would likely be deleting them soon, regardless. As a website, it was now a mess. Still, he wanted to hear the rest of what Mistress Jane had to say.

Rn-TLC: Oh! But now I wish to live here forever! In a single room in this very house. I could spend my days exploring each and every volume in this splendid library. Like a naughty child in a sweet shop, I have taken a lick from only a few of the books, but they leave me famished for more. Some were exactly what I desired, and some were like tasting anise for the first time. I shall read more of Mister Keats, Lord Byron, and Mister Pope and seek out their peers. I was surprised and gentled by Mistress Dickenson, and Mister Frost. Mistresses Plath and Bishop were a shock, as were Misters Eliot and Pound.

I know not why I chose those volumes from the dozens of other poets, but I now see that there has been a strange divergence of poetry from the forms that I know and love. Oh, give me a sonnet or a love poem any time. But poems of madness or madhouses, wandering streets or ponderous rantings? I am too set in my ways to understand, but it seems that in the world there is more verse written in the like of what the person in this house writes than there is of my beloved form. Perhaps I am not ready for this. Perhaps I have gone too far. When I was briefly in the land of Haida Gwaii, I heard their marvelous and dreamlike poems of man and the world of their spirits, and the Tamil had long chants and poems of devotion to their lords Vishnu and Shiva. In the land of the Mongol, I heard the chants to Lord Buddha, and in The Middle Kingdom, the beautiful, simple poetry of nature.

Perhaps I have come too far, but now I do appreciate some of the reasons this person has written in the manner that he does. This is common. It is normal for here. Scattershot piercings. Foggy solidity. Languid immediacy. Now I am writing like he does. Now I am beginning to understand.

Ron was feeling somewhat redeemed by the time he'd finished reading this section. Somewhat.

Chapter 30.

READING THIS last post had also raised some questions, and Ron leaned back in his chair as he considered the possibilities. *Just how long had Mistress Jane lived here? From what she's posted, it seems as if she's lived in our house for days, or perhaps weeks. It would take time to explore the house, read through my entire blog, write out her postings and compose that poem, any of which seem to have long stretches between them. And for her to be able to read all of those poets? And why doesn't she respond to any of the comments my friends have made between her posts? Does she not see them?*

"Ron?"

"Yeah?" Ron spun around to find Sara holding onto the doorframe.

"Do you wonder why we were chosen?"

Ron looked momentarily confused, but then said, "I guess I haven't thought about it."

"I mean, if it is at all real, why were you there to meet a young Will and at the same time someone you met there was here—seemingly with me in this house? Why us? Does that happen to everyone?"

"I would think not. And reading these postings by Mistress Jane, it sounds as if this was the first time for her in this century, too. I have no idea why."

"Well, I've been thinking that it must have had some purpose for you, since no one else knew you were even there. And it had some purpose for Mistress Jane, since none of us knew she was here. What do you think your reason for being there could be?"

Ron thought for a moment. "I suppose I learned to appreciate what I have more and to focus on myself less. And the value of simply being able to create..." Then he recalled something. "You know, I never mentioned this and nearly forgot, but there is just the slimmest chance that I helped John save Will."

"What? How is that?"

"I can never be sure, but you know how I had no ability to do anything other than watch John live his life? Right at the end, John was walking away from where Will was being attacked, and after I heard the highwaymen signal each other, I absolutely screamed at him to turn around. It was then that he hesitated and finally turned back to make sure Will was all right. It could be that I got through to him, but he could also have just acted on his own."

Sara nodded. "So, there might have been some reason. How about for Mistress Jane?"

"No idea yet. This travelling happens to her whenever she has a fit, and she says that she always seems to wind up in the place where a poet is. So maybe that was it."

"OK, you said to let you know if I thought of anything, so that was it. Oh, by the way, did you remember to pack my medications?"

"Oops," said Ron, and walked with her to the TV area before he headed upstairs to pack their toiletries and make sure that he hadn't forgotten anything else. On his way back into the study, it occurred to him that he had a huge volume of *The Collected Works of William Shakespeare* sitting on the bottom shelf of their little library. *I wonder if she ever noticed that? Now, that would have given her quite a shock.*

And it became immediately apparent that Mistress Jane had, indeed, noticed that same thing when Ron woke his computer.

Rn-TLC: I am seldom at a loss for words, but now I find myself so and struggle to find them again. I previously said that I must never tell about my journeys when I return from my spells, but now it is vital that I must never reveal what I know of the future. For now I know that this is the future. I also know something too precious. I was in the library and a large book on the bottom shelf caught my eye. It was not just one poem, or one play, but it was an entire collection of plays and poems. Each and every one written by my very own nephew. My precious Will. I now know that he will write. That he will write well. That his works will live on for a time far beyond my reckoning.

And such plays! Such sonnets! I could not help myself. I read them. Every one!

Oh, my god! thought Ron, *she must have been here for days just to read that one book! I still don't understand how this works—unless John's experience was just like Sara's. Unaware and at the bottom of the stairs the whole time. But does that mean that I was really manipulating John without knowing it? It makes no sense.*

Rn-TLC: They are perfect. They are how I believe poems should be written. And the plays are people I know. That bothersome butcher at the market in Stratford is Shylock. My neighbor Sarah's husband, Donald, is Iago. My own husband is surely Leonato. My husband's cousin John is Bottom, or I myself am an ass. But is it vanity or blindness? I cannot find myself in any of his plays. If it is vanity, I might be Lady MacBeth. If it is blindness, I might be Titania. But perhaps I sparked no inspiration. Perhaps I am too like him to evoke a character that is other than us. The writers.

Oh, I am so proud. To know that Will Shakespeare will grow into himself. That he will know our history. That he will give voice to our heroes, will speak for the commoner and the king. That he will have watched all of us so closely that anyone who sees his plays will find some part of themselves reflected. They will see their neighbors, their friends and their enemies. And that he will have such a sweet, touching voice in his poetry. That he will elevate every word. Oh, I am so proud to know him. My little Will.

Ron found himself suddenly uncomfortable, and he wasn't entirely sure why. He paged up and reread this last part, trying to pinpoint the cause of his unease. They were all words of praise for her nephew, and she seemed to have been elated to have read his works. Still there was something that bothered him. He gave a mental shrug and continued reading what followed.

Rn-TLC: I feel that I am about to return home. I cannot see anyone yet, but I heard my maid whispering over my bedside a moment ago, and I can smell the lavender drops she likes to rub into my neck.

I do not know why I have decided to set down my thoughts, my diary, here, in this picture frame. It is as if it were both a startlingly new practice and yet a familiar old habit at the same time. As if this was what one does here—makes expressions, shares thoughts, communicates even when unable to see another person. And it is so deliciously easy. The words fly up to the frame—a lark set free out of a cage.

I want to reveal something of myself... but to whom? This will go out to those I do not know, those who usually read his words. Or, perhaps they disappear in the ether. Regardless, I want to impart that I have learned something in my strange travels. It may not be how things are, but it is as I see them. At home, such things must not be spoken of, but I will not be here long and can leave this behind without any fear of recrimination. Much as a dying man can feel free to utter his innermost thoughts and desires.

This goes against all of my Christian upbringing and I know it is blasphemous, but I know now that we can be in many places and times all at once. If this was not so, how can I be here imparting these words and also hearing my maid's worried mutterings as if she's in the very next room? Otherwise, this could not have happened to me more often than can be believed.

We are also many people at once, although this is something I sense more than I know. Not only that, but we are many different living things at once. Do you wonder why a butterfly should choose to land on your hand? Why an unfamiliar cat will come up and rub your leg? They are all you. They enjoy seeing you enjoying them and interacting with them. And your best friends and worst enemies? Many of them are you engaged in a large play about your many selves. Each is you in a different role, all at once.

I also believe this about life. We are not aware of it, but we have followed both paths at every fork in the road that we have ever chanced. Every critical event happened both ways. Yes, you were hit by that carriage that just missed you last year. You did catch the plague from that night in a barn where you saw the rats. But you also married every one of the gentlemen or maidens you fancied. You wrote that book or the play which seemed beyond your abilities. You discovered something marvelous about yourself and the world. Don't despair. You are in a huge mosaic and can only see one piece at each moment, but you did it all. You ranged far and added something precious of yourself in each journey.

And that was the end of her postings. Ron had long forgotten his unease from the previous section and now had the sense that, for a brief moment, he'd been subtly lifted out of his body. *I wasn't expecting anything remotely like this out of her,* he thought in wonder. *If I'm to believe what she's written, living in different places and times—some de-*

tails of which she could have no way of knowing if she was ensconced in her Welford home in Elizabethan England—then she might not be merely a victim of epilepsy, but go through something much more profound while under her spells. And now this last bit—she's had a religious experience of some sort. I could assume it was her seizures if this were all in her head and she was relating her experiences to someone back home. But she was here, *and that is certainly not living in her own head. Is it?*

Chapter 31.

THE LIGHT was fading, and the traffic had slowed due to the intermittent snow squalls. They'd spent the first twenty minutes discussing the mind-boggling possibilities of time travel and multi-body habitation and had then fallen into their own thoughts. The signal from WORT had whispered into static and Sara, keeping her head as still as possible, reached over and switched off the radio. They drove in silence for several minutes more and were approaching Mineral Point when Sara turned slightly toward him and asked, "What is it, Ron?"

"What?"

"What's bugging you? You're not going to be in one of your funks while we're with my mom and dad, are you?"

Ron took his eyes off the road for a second and gave her a smile. "Nope, I was just thinking."

They'd driven for a mile more when Ron said, "Did you know that John Keats asked that 'Here lies one whose name was writ on water,' be inscribed on his gravestone? And that his granite grave marker doesn't even bear his name, just 'young English poet' as a reference to him?'"

"No, I didn't," said Sara, without asking what had brought this up.

"Isn't that ironic? His name wasn't written in stone, and he tells us that it is written on water instead. Was he being really clever by asking that his name not be inscribed on his gravestone—to drive the point home? Or did he ask for that quote because he thought, incorrectly as it turns out, that his poetry and his name wouldn't stand the test of time? He was unappreciated when he died, but he was so young that lack of fame at that age is to be expected."

They glanced at each other. The look from Sara asked where this was going, and the look from Ron said that he had more to tell.

"OK, so that NPR piece on speculation about next year's Pulitzer Prize winners got me thinking about John Kennedy Toole. Remember him? We both loved *A Confederacy of Dunces*?"

"Of course, I remember the book; it was great. And he also died young, right?"

"Yeah, but what I was getting at is that he won that Pulitzer only years later. His book wasn't even published when he committed suicide, and he might have done it because it wasn't published. And Emily Dickenson, William Blake, and many others were also obscure when they died."

A different look from Sara needed no words.

"No, Honey. I'm not trying to compare myself to all those famous authors. I'm realizing that there is a whole spectrum of writers out there, and there always has been. There are those who are deservedly famous for what they've written when they are alive, and those who become appreciated after they are gone. But, there are also those who are incredibly good and never get recognized, those who are so-so and do get recognized, but only for a short time, and on down the spectrum."

Ron stole another quick glance at Sara. "You know that I wanted to get my poems out there. I thought they were good enough to stand up against other's works."

"They are good, Ron, and you and I both know it."

"Yeah, but how do they stack up with the readers, and where do they fit in the universe of poetry? Sure, I wanted to be included in a collection some time, or maybe get some kind of accolade, but I now get it that it's out of my hands. That's what Kristen was trying to tell me years ago with her paper boats on a lake analogy. And like what I told you earlier about what Mistress Jane had written on my blog. Writing is really just about the writing. I can relax. That doesn't mean that I can just throw the words out there slapdash—I have to write as if there will be an audience, maybe, sometime. I need to keep putting the effort into it—a lot of effort—so that the writing itself is transparent and doesn't get in the way of the poetry. But I can do that now honestly with zero expectations—something I'd lied to myself about before. Just like thousands of others. Just as long as I don't lose the spark, the urge to create something, I'll be content."

Sara reached over and patted his shoulder.

He took the pat as a 'yeah, sure,' kind of pat.

"I know, I know. It's my ego, right?" nodded Ron. "You think I'm just saying the words but will soon be back to writing my publishing rants, and my 'what an unfair world' whining. I know it's a problem for me, but I think I've really moved on. In fact, I'm planning on deleting all of the non-poetry off my website because I'm not going back there. And my Rite of Rejection is a thing of the past. Honest."

Sara suddenly laughed, but Ron could hear immediately that it wasn't in derision. Even so, he peeked at her, just to make sure. "Hey, I was agreeing with you and being supportive," she clarified with a grin. They both stared at the beautiful dark winter landscape as they neared the border with Illinois. "And I love the direction you're heading."

"We're heading," nodded Ron.

Chapter 32.

SARA AND her mom were in the sewing room which also served as a study, examining wedding gowns they found on the internet. Sara had insisted that she didn't want to wear anything other than the nice party dress that she'd picked out, but Gladys was dead set on a gown for the occasion. Pete and Ron were in the living room with Pete half-heartedly watching the Bears on TV, and Ron not watching at all, thumbing idly through a coffee table book about the kings and queens of England he'd grabbed from the well-polished chairside table. He'd begun reading and researching more about England in the Elizabethan Era—with the vague notion of a novel in mind.

"God, I don't even know half of these players anymore, and I used to worship those guys. The Fridge, McMahon, Payton—you know?" asked Pete.

Ron nodded. "Same with me and the Packers. Aaron Rogers and a few, but the others? And this season is even worse for me knowing who's on the team." Not much of a football fan, Ron had punted on this.

"Then, I'm not alone," nodded Pete. "Thought it might just be me getting too old. I mean, Ditka is the last coach I really remember. And I live in Illinois, for Christ's sakes."

There was some action on the television which distracted them, but the refs got involved and a series of fouls allowed each to drift back into their own spaces for a spell.

Then Pete shifted in his chair so that he was facing Ron more directly. "Say, Ron," Ron looked over at Pete with raised eyebrows. "I just wanted you to know how happy we are that you and Sara are making it official. It will be good to have you as a bona fide member of the family."

"Thanks, Pete. That means a lot."

Pete looked momentarily at a loss for words, but then said, "You know, I need to apologize for something."

"What could that possibly be, Pete?" asked Ron.

"Well, I don't know if you could tell, but I've been sort of holding you at arm's length the whole time you've been with Sara. I know that she loves you and that you love her, but I was never positive that it would last."

"I sure hope that it will," said Ron.

"Yeah, I'm sure it will. But after she was so taken with Nathan, and he got so close to us—well, after she and him broke up after it looked like they would be together for-ever, well, it sort of took the wind out of my sails. I felt like I couldn't see investing in anyone if they weren't going to last. You know what I'm saying?"

Ron felt that he did know what Pete was saying, and it explained a lot. "Yeah, I think I do." There was some more silence between the two while the crowd roared from the TV. "You know, it might not have been just because of Nathan, and you might have picked up on it." said Ron.

Now it was Pete's turn to make a curious face.

"I hate to admit it, but until recently, I can see that I didn't take Sara seriously enough. I mean, sure, I love her, and always have, but I think I took her for granted. I didn't really realize what I had."

Pete's expression was now unreadable.

"But now suddenly, I see that she's the best thing that has or ever will happen to me. Literally the absolute best thing. And I will never let her go."

Now Pete smiled and nodded. "She is the best, isn't she?"

"Yeah, the very best."

Chapter 33.

AFTER THAT evening, Ron got on famously with Sara's parents. Ron didn't even mind going to the two seasonal parties her folks had RSVP'd, as long as Sara was comfortable with her bandages and the puffy purple-green rings around her eyes, and he thoroughly enjoyed the Christmas Eve gathering her parents put on. Christmas itself was, thankfully, low-key, as were the two days that followed, after which they were to head home. The day before they left, Ron found himself alone in the house. Sara and Gladys had gone out to do some shopping, wandering up and down the colorful main street that ran along the river and below Galena's bluff, and Pete had driven to a physical therapy appointment and then to a weekly get-together with some pals at a local tavern. Ron had offered to drive, but Pete had insisted that he drove slow enough that any accident could avoid him.

For the first time since their arrival, Ron visited his blogsite. The holidays had engendered only a smattering of activity. At the bottom of the post were simple Christmas greetings from BL and StanzaGuru, to which he replied in kind.

And then, in a rare occasion, fingers poised at the keyboard, Ron realized that he had nothing to add to his site. He scanned through the posts left by Mistress Jane, reread the last two essays he'd written on the publishing process, went through some of his latest poems, and finally skimmed the comments. He sat back and let the overall impression of his website sink in, and he found himself still staring at the screen after five minutes of doing so.

It's time for a change, he finally decided. *Time for me to change.*

First, he altered the settings on the webpages so that comments were no longer accepted. He still wanted contact with anyone who read his works, but he thought it better for the exchanges to be conducted in a less public manner. To this end, he made sure that the Contact Me page was updated and could accept messages from anyone, except robots. Deleting all the comments took more time than he expected because they were so scattered throughout his blogs. Some were touching and it was difficult to erase them, but there were many he wiped out with great satisfaction. He had a much harder time when it came to deleting his rants. *It felt so good to write them out, and some of them were even pretty damn on target, but they gotta go if this is going to be a website focused on poetry,* he thought as he highlighted each one in turn and sent them all to the trash.

Finally, Ron wanted to save all the sections written by Mistress Jane, but not keep them on his website, and he took his time in highlighting them. He clicked 'copy,' then opened a blank document on his computer and clicked 'paste.' Nothing happened. He set his cursor at the top of the blank document and tried again. Nothing. *I must not have clicked on 'copy' in the first place,* he thought. He went back to the website, and instead of highlighted text, there were blank spaces. The text had disappeared. "Shit!" yelled Ron, just as Gladys and Sara opened the main door after returning from their shopping trip.

"Ron!" admonished Gladys.

"What happened, Ron?" asked Sara.

Ron was trying everything that came to mind as they entered the living room. When Sara came up beside him, she remained quiet as she watched him, clicking 'undo,' trying 'paste' in several documents, on the desktop, and on his website; searching the trash bin; pounding on the wooden desktop. When he finally leaned back and craned his neck up to her with a defeated look on his face, she gently asked, "What was it, Ron?"

"Everything that Mistress Jane wrote on my website is gone. It just disappeared. I highlighted it and then tried to copy it to my computer, but I must have hit the wrong thing by mistake. It's vapor."

She squeezed his shoulder. "Isn't there something you can do? Some kind of recovery?"

Ron was shaking his head. "Nope, I never created a backup copy and the only thing I can do is to pray that the web host made one automatically while her stuff was up. I don't have the passwords with me to check, but I'm not holding out much hope."

"Ah, I'm sorry, Babe."

"Yeah, me, too..." He stared out in front of him. "But isn't it weird, and maybe a little creepy? I read the poem she wrote for Will on actual paper, and that seems to have disappeared, and now somehow all of what she wrote about being in our house is gone, too. Shit."

A faint "Ron!" came from another end of the house.

"Sorry!" he yelled back.

Sara thought for a moment. "You know what I would do? Especially if there was no backup?" He turned to her again and raised his eyebrows. "I'd write down everything you can remember about what she wrote—even the exact wording if you can. Otherwise, that will go too, quicker than you might think."

Ron did just that, and they brought him dinner as he was still typing until late into the night.

Chapter 34.

Sara read Ron's reconstruction of Mistress Jane's writings during the drive back to Madison. Balancing his laptop on her knees, she would ask questions or give mild exclamations as she progressed. "Wow, Ron," she said, closing the cover when she was finished. "What do you think of that? It would never have occurred to me that someone with epilepsy would be somewhere else when they were having an episode."

"I have no idea what happens when someone's having a seizure," said Ron, keeping his eyes on the road. "I just assumed it was epilepsy, but maybe it was something else?"

"Whatever it was, it was more than just a dream or a vision on her part. I mean she even described her—me—using our toilet!"

"I know," said Ron. "And remember, I'm convinced that I really was in Welford. It was so tangible, and I met people that I couldn't possibly have known anything about unless I was there."

"And you had the written account that she was here," with an inflection showing regret that it no longer existed. Ron's minor grimace showed that he was now mostly resigned to the fact.

Ron thought for a while and then posited, "How about this? I was knocked out for maybe a few minutes on the ice and was suddenly living with John who had woken up from a fall, and I was there for maybe a week in those few moments. Mistress Jane went into a trance and maybe woke up with you who also had a fall. And then... well I'm not sure how it all worked, but isn't it strange that four people lost consciousness at around the same time and two of us switched locations—minds? bodies? I mean something happened."

"Something sure did, but again, why don't I remember anything?"

"You said you had a dream about reading a book of poetry in our house? Mistress Jane described that, too, so at least you did remember something. And John obviously wasn't aware I was there at all, so he would remember nothing..."

"But we have no real proof that any of this happened, do we? I mean, you certainly couldn't bring anything back with you, and all of the evidence we had about Mistress Jane has disappeared—the written poem, the postings."

"What about the washrag, and the beans?"

"What beans?" asked Sara, and Ron reminded her of Mistress Jane's description of a can and of the possibility of an extra one in the recycle bin.

"Oof, this is too much to think about," Sara leaned back against the headrest and closed her eyes. She almost whispered, "And the part about us being many different people at once... Are you sure you remember that right?"

Ron didn't answer, so she opened an eye and looked over at him to find him nodding. She continued, "I don't know if I can wrap my head around that, much less her other ideas. She seemed like your normal everyday time or space traveler until I read that. Now I think she was either nuts or some kind of enlightened sage or something."

Ron was still nodding. "I think I caught the gist of what she wrote, but I could have missed something. You know, when I first read that part in my blog, it seemed so true that I felt like I was transported somewhere else for a moment. It's hard to describe, but somehow it seemed like she was absolutely right on. It sort of made sense to me, but now I'm more—iffy."

The car was silent for several miles, until WORT radio came back into range.

Chapter 35.

Both Ron and Sara had a few days before going back to their day jobs at the start of the new year, and they enjoyed every moment of them. Sara even loved being recovered enough that she could go into work on the 29th when the hospital was short-staffed and desperately needed her help. Ron had cleaned up his website and given it a more polished and professional appearance—because he'd decided that he wanted to be more professional himself. He even had Sara take a picture with him posed in front of their bookcase and staring somewhat pensively off into the distance. He added this photograph to the About Me tab with a vague sense of hypocrisy after the rant he'd mentally composed while in England.

Looking over his site, he felt the need to explain the changes he'd made in it to those who had stuck with him. Under his welcoming banner, he wrote the following:

Some of you who have visited here in the past will notice changes in this website. While I have benefited from the feedback provided to my poems, I have decided to discontinue comments. I will miss the immediate camaraderie, but still welcome any feedback or communication through my contact page. I have also deleted all of my prose essays.

Why this change? My website was too similar to me as a person, and not enough like me as a poet. The previous version provided a place for me to publicly vent, and simultaneously provided one for the rest of you to do the same. This felt good, but in the end, I find that it detracted from the poetry, which will be my sole focus from here on out.

I now understand that in all of my poems I've written: me. I've had no other choice. It's how I see beautiful/ugly normal/weird sad/happy; it's how I feel an interminably long and dreary doldrum or a lightning-flash frozen-frame moment; it's how sometimes words just suddenly appear on the pages and when edited, stay the same. This means that what others say about them won't change them in the slightest. You can't put toothpaste back in the tube. When it comes down to it, I write my own reality. If you're not happy with it, please go write your own. Go sing it, dance it, pray it, play it. In the end, those of us trying to form something out of empty nothingness, are doing the best that we can. Attempting to pin opinion on something made of airy nothing is futile. The best rejoinder will be you composing your own haiku or couplet. Then we're talking.

Chapter 36.

Ron hadn't written much new poetry since before the holidays and had focused instead on editing those poems he'd sketched out in the past. He'd been busy cleaning house all day in preparation for some friends they were having over the next evening to celebrate New Year's Eve with a meal. Sara's eyes still wore a greenish yellow mask which she found she could cover up with some makeup she rarely used, so she wasn't too embarrassed for company. All the while Ron was vacuuming, he was thinking about his experience in England, and of Mistress Jane's time spent in their house. In a philosophical mood, he stopped his work and wrote down a poem so that it wouldn't be immediately forgotten, but one that he doubted would make it onto his webpage.

> When I was young, I would fry in the sun.
> My shedding skin always obliging with a replacement.
> I'd wondered if we were snakes in disguise
> And I kept close watch on my body for signs.
> Later, I turned my eyes to the layers of my being,
> Enamored with the idea of slowly peeling them away,
>   like an onion.
> I imagined strip-mining deeper for the core until—
>   there was no more.
> But now I see I had it wrong—I'm really the worm of
>   self-discovery.
> I worked hard at getting through the first layer, but
>   everything remained dark.
> The entire weight of my being was not made much
>   lighter.

I'm working from the inside out.
The inner layer was tiny, and it seemed like such an
    effort at the time.
But once gone, I had more space filled with what I
    knew.
Each layer is larger, takes more time, becomes a little
    tougher,
But some light starts to show through—
I have expanded the amount of self I know.
Someday, I'll finally reach that thin but extremely
    tough outer surface.
There will be little nutrition and furious effort at the
    end.
I'll be starved and exhausted,
But my small space will finally join that greater
    expanse.

Ms. Skarsgaard had phoned that she was ready to come over, so Ron had met her at her front door to help carry her Parker House rolls and give her support for the trek next door to his house. It wasn't slippery, and she did fine, but Ron somehow still enjoyed walking with her affectionate arm tucked up tight against him.

"Brrr," she said. "But it's not as cold as it was in the late '70's. Do you remember those coupla years, Ronald? I think you musta been five or so. Our pipes froze up but good, and we spent the day and that night at your house. Your parents were always so kind to us."

"No, I don't really remember," replied Ron.

He was just about to correct her about his age when she added, "No, you were more like two or three. You kept toddling after Lars. I remember now."

In his mind, the coldest winter he'd ever spent was the winter his mother had died, but he didn't say so as they made it up the steps to his porch and safely inside.

"Hello, Ms. Skarsgaard," said his uncle Paul in greeting as he and Aunt Natalie came over to help her with her coat.

"Well, Paul, so nice to see you," while taking his arm, and the three of them wandered over to the sofa to catch up.

Sara's friend Maggie and her husband had joined them, and Toby had been invited as well.

Ron felt like it was him instead of the turkey that got roasted as they sat around the table eating a Thanksgiving-style potluck, but he didn't mind one bit. Ms. Skarsgaard kicked it off with a few shady tales of Ron's early teens. Uncle Paul told some stories of Ron's first years partying when he'd moved into this big house by himself—and what a change Sara had made in his life soon after. And Toby couldn't resist retelling hijinks from their university days. In the end, Ron felt like a felon who'd received clemency for good behavior, which was probably not far from the truth.

Ron had seen Ms. Skarsgaard home, and his uncle and Natalie were getting ready to leave when Paul pulled him aside. "Ron, I like what you've done with your website," he said.

"Thanks, Uncle Paul. I thought it needed cleaning up."

"Not only that, but it's also much more polished looking now. I think visitors would be impressed."

"Well, I've had a change of attitude lately. I was going to shut it down, but decided to make a more serious effort instead."

"And it shows. It makes people take your poetry more seriously, too. You really should join me at that conference in Ames, you know. There are several workshops that you'd find very interesting, and you can read some examples of your own writing in them, too. It would be great exposure, and an easy way to network with some regional poets. Have you given it any more thought?"

"As a matter of fact, I have. I was going to ask you if you minded me tagging along," thinking that he would also need to call Nathan since he'd decided to accept his offer of joining him on part of his tour.

"Not at all, Ron," said Paul with a grin. "I'd welcome the company on the drive down. I have a friend I'm sure we can stay with, and we can make plans."

"Thanks so much, I'm actually looking forward to it," said Ron, reaching out to shake his uncle's hand, something they rarely did.

Sara joined him in the living room just as he hung up after his call to Nathan.

"Well, look at you," said Sara when he'd ended the call. "Wonnie is all gwoed up!" giving him a dig in the ribs as she said it.

"Stop!" he laughed as he grabbed her.

"No, really, Hon. It's like you suddenly realize that you're just as good as any of the others out there."

Ron pulled his head back and gave her a doubtful look.

"Okay, as good as many others out there," she corrected.

"Now that's possible," he said, releasing her from his hug. "And it's also a matter of not caring as much about what others think. It's like the simple act of taking my website more seriously has made me committed to this writing path. Or maybe it was the other way around. Either way, it feels so natural for me to be doing this. This is who I am, so I may as well recognize it and embrace it."

"Like I embrace you," as she dove in for another hug.

He knew it seemed like a cheesy moment, but Ron squeezed her all the more tightly for it.

❧

Ron sat down at his computer after they'd finished washing the dishes from the potluck and tried to view his webpages with the eye of a visitor as Paul had intimated. He found that the site wasn't half bad from that perspective. Then, at the end of the section devoted to his most recent poems, Ron noticed entries written in a familiar style that wasn't his own. *Now, how did I miss this?* He wondered. The time stamp indicated that it had been posted just recently, which made no sense at all because he had blocked any ability for the public to comment. And Sara, in this case, was considered to be public.

Rn-TLC: I return here? I have been exhausted and must have fallen again into my spell. Never have I set foot in the same place twice, so this is strange, indeed. The spell is not deep this time. I hear them worry over my bedside.

I have read again what I had imparted before, and I must let it be known that I am of another mind about my nephew. Alas, I now realize that I can write no more poetry. Or, if I do, I can never share it with young Will. I have read his verses. I have read his plays. What if I unintentionally write some of his own words? What if I use one of his conceits? One of his rhymes? Might he then not use them so as to not copy me? Or I might get the idea just wrong enough that it would change how he would use it. Oh, this is the saddest day. I must kill the most dearest exchange I have ever had with another living person.

Reading this, Ron immediately remembered the uneasy feeling he'd had on learning that Mistress Jane had read her own nephew's collected works. *This was why—she could change history!* he realized, praying that her effects on Will wouldn't alter anything in the past. *But why is this here?* Was his more immediate concern. *Is she on Sara's laptop right now?* He was about to stand up and check on Sara. *Or maybe this makes sense if I missed this when I accidentally erased all of Mistress Jane's entries. But if so, why is the timestamp from today?*

Then it came to him. *And she has reread what she blogged before? Where, for Christ's sake? I accidentally deleted them... at least I thought I had.* He quickly scanned all his other posted pages for entries he might have overlooked and found nothing, and then rechecked his entire website, including the deleted files folder, with the same result. Another surprise awaited when he returned to that strange posting by Mistress Jane—it had changed while he was away.

> Rn-TLC: The chances are just as good that I am supposed to have read his works and carry that knowledge with me when I next meet with Will. I will need to be careful, but perhaps it is our sharing of poems that leads him on to his destiny. Perhaps if I halt these wonderful exchanges, he will halt his writing. I would then have committed a great sin against him and his legacy. There is no doubt that I must continue to encourage and help this beautiful boy in any way possible. I am the luckiest aunt in the entire world.
> Oh! Sweet Apothecary! He has given me...

What? He has given you what? Ron wondered while at the same time being glad of her change of heart. He waited several minutes for another entry, but none came. He was about to touch a key on his keyboard when he froze with the realization that anything he did would likely cause this entry to evaporate. *If I try to copy it, it will probably vaporize like the last time; if I switch to another page, it is likely to change or vanish...* "Hey, Sara? Could you come here?" he called out.

"Sure, just a sec," she replied. And then, "What's up?" as she walked up behind him.

"Have you been on your laptop just now?" he asked.

"Nope, I've been reading that cozy mystery about the candlemaker I told you about. Why?"

"Just so you know that I haven't been making all of this up, could you read this paragraph?"

Sara read over his shoulder. "Are you kidding? So, this is from Mistress Jane? From my laptop? I thought her posts had all disappeared."

"They had—and I've disallowed comments. Look at the timestamp."

"That's like a minute ago," she said confused. "How could that be? I haven't been near my computer and I haven't..."

"Haven't what?"

"Well, it's possible?"

"What's possible?"

"Well, if Mistress Jane was here somehow... I did fall asleep for a few minutes while I was reading my book—it's been such a long day. She can't just jump into someone who's sleeping. Can she?"

"I have absolutely no idea," replied Ron. "But right now, I need to know how to save this." He explained all the possible ways this might disappear and asked if she had any thoughts about how to try and preserve it.

"It's short, so let's write it down first," she suggested.

Ron copied the paragraph out in longhand, and then Sara said, "Oh, duh. Take a picture with your cell phone."

Ron gave her a look that said 'now you tell me' and then did as she suggested. "Ok, but how do we save the original?"

"Copying won't work?" she asked. Ron shook his head at this. "What if you try a screen capture?"

"How do I do that?"

"I think you hold down the Windows key, and the Print Screen key at the same time."

"Are you sure?"

"Yep. I'm almost positive—here let me look it up on my phone just to be safe," said Sara, and was soon able to confirm that this was the proper procedure.

Ron followed those directions, and the screen momentarily dimmed as the instructions said it should. The paragraph was gone when the screen relit, while the poem just above it remained. "What the…?" he shouted.

"Look in your most recent pictures folder, Ron. It should be there."

"Shit!" said Ron and Sara in unison when the opened screen print revealed the last poem on the page with a blank space beneath it.

"Oh, shit again!' said Ron as he stood up.

"What?" asked Sara.

"I've gotta check something," Ron replied as he headed for their small library.

He went to the bookcase and pulled out *The Collected Works of William Shakespeare* and began leafing through the pages. To his great relief, everything was as he'd remembered.

Chapter 37.

A WEEK later, Ron found himself wondering again if Mistress Jane had decided to continue working with William, and what the outcome had been. He'd searched all of the historical literature that he could get his hands on and found no mention of a connection between Mistress Jane and Will, other than through genealogy. This did not surprise him, since this lack of information was to be expected after a passage of some four hundred-plus years. As to the impact the knowledge from her visit to the twenty-first century might have had on her nephew, he accepted that he would never know, but that didn't stop him from thinking about it.

He had reread some of his favorite Shakespearean sonnets to see if any had changed, and it seemed that none had. Neither had any of the famous quotations he could recall from The Bard's plays. However, after going through the myriad possibilities that messing with timelines suggested, he was also aware that if Shakespeare's writings had been modified, history itself would have been altered, and his works would be as Ron now remembered them anyway. *Another intriguing puzzle,* he said to himself, continuing to solder the maze of circuits that others might have considered to be equally mystifying.

Toby was out for the afternoon—on 'pressing business' of some sort, and Stew was whistling happily away above the strains of *Baba O'Riley* by The Who coming out loud over the speakers. Holding the wire from a capacitor in place with needle-nose pliers, Ron waited patiently while this one and the wire it was to be mated with were hot enough for the solder to flow evenly, finally satisfied when it did so.

Ron, as usual, became unaware of the actual task at hand as he pondered Mistress Jane's dilemma born from knowing the future while living in the past. He had been uneasy at the prospect of her somehow affecting the writings of her nephew, given what she had learned by reading Will's plays and sonnets in their library. Suddenly remembering the first poem written by Mistress Jane and the familiar sounding phrases in it, he realized that she may have had an influence on the boy long before her trip to twenty-first century Madison. If this was the case, Will was in careful, nurturing hands.

Ron then wondered about Mistress Jane's conjecture that multiple outcomes came from each choice we made. Was it possible she had decided to encourage Will along one timeline and to quit sharing poetry with him along another? He loved Shakespeare just the way it was, and it bothered him that there could be different variations floating about on the other possible timelines. His thoughts began to spread out along them.

What if we're on the wrong timeline, and don't have the exact words as Will set them down? had just crossed his mind when he propped his soldering iron in its stand. *Don't be ridiculous, Ron,* and *No, I don't need to worry about her affecting anything at all,* quickly followed on the heels of this. He sat for a spell staring into space, and then, coming to a resolution and grabbing his handy notebook, he wrote down his final thoughts on the matter.

Altering Time

Sci-Fi writers stay your pens.
Theoretical physicists halt your pondering.

For I have proof irrefutable
That the Universe is immutable.
Our timeline flies as true as an arrow—
And here is my theorem in case you're wondering:
Could there exist a world in which—
There is no caucus of ravens on an alien shore,
And the raven did not quote 'nevermore'?
Birnam Wood did not remove to Dunsinane
and two roads never diverged in a yellow wood?
No one cut and peeled a hazel wand,
Or measured out their life with coffee spoons?
No one stood a tiptoe and was roused at the name of
    Crispian?
Or, could there ever be a world to live in
Where all your sounds of woe were not converted
Into hey, nonny, nonny?
No?
Neither do I believe so.
Ergo, in sum,
Quod erat demonstrandum

Chapter 38.

AMES WAS no warmer than Madison, but Ron had enjoyed his evening walk through an unfamiliar neighborhood just the same. He and Paul had arrived in the late afternoon and were welcomed into the home of a close friend of Paul's. Darrin was also a professor of English Literature at Iowa State University, and he and Paul had met in grad school. The Knapp's hospitality was overwhelming. Darrin's wife, Simone, had shown them around the house, gotten them settled into their rooms, and then had served up a cheese platter with some white wine while, in the meantime, Darrin had cooked up a fabulous dinner of several Creole dishes.

When he returned from his after-dinner stroll, the lighting in the house was subdued, and Ron found his uncle, Darrin, and Simone sitting before a glass-faced woodstove insert set within the space of the former fireplace. Paul was reaching over to clink glasses with Darrin as Ron took the fourth seat, immediately enjoying the warmth from the fire. Ron had expected their expressions to be more upbeat for a toast, but they looked dour instead. Or perhaps it was the lighting.

"Would you like a scotch, Ron?" asked Simone.

Not being much of a hard liquor fan, Ron asked, "Maybe some tea? I can get it."

"No, no, you need to warm up. I'd be happy to get it. Black or herbal?"

"Herbal would be great. Thanks."

"My pleasure," said Simone as she rose to fetch him a cup.

"Why the long faces?" asked Ron, hoping that he wasn't, yet again, misreading the situation.

Paul looked over and gave him a brave half-smile. "We were just drinking to the death of the Humanities," he said.

"Related to the talk we had in the car?" asked Ron, with Paul nodding in reply.

"Simone was just telling us that the language courses she teaches are still doing relatively well, but that several of the French literature classes may not have enough enrollees to survive another semester."

Paul had been the most candid Ron had seen him on the drive down to Iowa State University. He had told Ron that one of the five English literature courses he taught was being dropped next year, and attendance had been trending down in the other courses over the last ten years. He had said that he wasn't particularly worried about his position since he was tenured, but that most English literature programs across the nation were scrambling to attract students.

At the time, Ron had wondered aloud whether the smartphone and television were taking the place of the printed page, meaning that interest in literature was fading. He had told his uncle about his own change in attitude about writing that was steering him away from published results, and they had then discussed the lack of sales Ron had seen, even though this was no longer a primary focus for him.

"Well," Paul had said, "from what I understand, you needn't worry too much about a lack of readership if you do attempt to market your poetry. The students I talk to are still reading. They just don't see any value in a Humanities degree. Everything is job-based now. It used to be that a broad education was a goal—being well read was expected or even celebrated. Now, if you don't know marketing and programming, you're not considered to be prepared for life. For them, 'literacy' means being up on the latest streaming content and podcasts."

He had then told Ron that he had fibbed a little about the real purpose for his trip. "I'm going to sit in on the poetry workshop if I get a chance, but the real reason I'm visiting is to attend some meetings with the ISU Lang and Lit professors to try and come up with a way to avert some drastic cuts they're facing. The monies flowing into land grant universities are being throttled, and they don't want their program to die."

Seeing the look of curiosity on Darrin's face at Ron's question about the car trip conversation, Ron then summarized the gist of it for him.

"Le sujet du jour," said Simone as she arrived with Ron's mug of tea. And then, "The topic of the day," in case Ron wasn't a French speaker.

The conversation around the fire for the next half hour was mainly about departmental woes. When that wound down, Ron asked about the best compositions they'd seen from their classes recently. The mood brightened considerably as the three professors lauded their star pupils and their hopes for the future of literature.

The sunshine the next morning was absolutely brilliant. Each twig on every tree was encrusted with crystalline frost, and Ron had barely been able to keep his eyes open from the reflected glare during his walk to the workshop on campus. As his uncle had assured him would be the case, Ron had been welcomed to attend the regional conference sponsored by the Midwest Writers Group and had been encouraged to read a few of his poems.

He was now sitting near the rear of the small hall—pitted out, drained, and yet fully engaged in the other readings. The critiques of the three poems he had read had been frank, insightful, biting, and encouraging, and he had learned something from each commenter. Mia Gonzales, a car factory worker's daughter attending Iowa State University from Detroit, was reading a poem about the freedom and power she had imagined she would inherit as a teenager that had been inspired by a hall pass she had rediscovered from the sixth grade. Her verses had a crisp urban edge that Ron found to be the opposite of his own writings, but captivating in their rhythm.

When Mia finished, they broke for coffee and pastries and Ron sat for a moment taking in the crowd. He was glad to see that he was far from the oldest non-student there, and he recognized the three famous regional poets, who had been introduced at the beginning of the session, now meeting near the podium. As the main stream of attendees headed toward the refreshments, a portion of them was breaking off to approach the trio and begin their expected hovering.

Ron suddenly found himself wondering what Mistress Jane would have made of the workshop. The literate in her day were limited mainly to members of the upper class. Here, there were people from a spectrum of backgrounds, presenting a multitude of ideas and images. Rather than to a privileged few, the waters from her creative founts were flowing through suburban garden hoses, farming irrigation ditches, clanking, rusting pipes, radiator hoses, glacial streams, and home taps to reach these poets. And he drank from the same waters. An odd feeling of belonging came over him, and he was glad that he now had the inner sense of security to embrace it. He made a mental note to assure his uncle that the wellsprings of poetry in the world were not subsiding anytime soon.

He'd liked most of the poems he'd heard so far that morning, but was particularly impressed by Mia's reading. He rose from his seat and went to seek her out. Her sudden, deft shift from a hall pass and pre-teen expectations to the Voting Rights Act and recent efforts to restrict it had stirred the entire room. The juxtaposition of a hall monitor and a self-appointed poll watcher was particularly effective. He wanted to both encourage her and to ask her if she had always written about socially relevant topics, or if it was part of a personal evolution. This poetry that sought to make a difference had never grabbed his attention as it had today, and he wanted to learn more about it, what it sprang from, and where it might take him.

ACKNOWLEDGEMENTS

I want to thank Lynn Ate for her suggestions and time spent in editing, and Jessica Hatch of Hatch Editorial Services for an editorial assessment that pointed me in new and better directions. The beta readers at Entrada Publishing also provided most welcome comments about the very rough first draft.

References from the final poem:

Conrad Aiken, *A Letter to Li Po*
Edgar Allen Poe, *The Raven*
William Shakespeare, *MacBeth*
Robert Frost, *The Road not Taken*
William Butler Yeats, *The Song of the Wandering Aengus*
T. S. Eliot, *The Lovesong of J. Alfred Prufrock*
William Shakespeare, *Henry V*
William Shakespeare, *Much Ado About Nothing*

ABOUT THE AUTHOR

David Ackley grew up in Fairbanks, Alaska and raised a family in Juneau. His professional career in Alaska included both fisheries biometrics and management positions with the state and federal governments. He has earned Master's degrees in Chinese Language and Literature (Wisconsin), and in Fisheries Science (Alaska). David is now retired and living in northern Idaho, where he began a small business in lutherie – building guitars, Irish bouzoukis, and ukuleles (www.dastringedinstruments.com). The lutherie business has flagged somewhat while he gets some stories out of his head. Please visit the Rain and Breeze Books website, www.rainandbreeze.com, for more information about David and his books.

www.ingramcontent.com/pod-product-compliance
Lightning Source LLC
Chambersburg PA
CBHW060815190726
48285CB00002B/672